Rotten Apple

Rotten Apple

Rebecca Eckler

Doubleday Canada

Doubleday Canada and colophon are trademarks

Library and Archives of Canada Cataloguing in Publication
has been applied for

ISBN: 978-0-385-66318-2

This book is a work of fiction. Names, characters, places and
incidents are products of the author's imagination or are used
fictitiously. Any resemblance to actual events or locales or
persons, living or dead, is entirely coincidental.

Book design: Leah Springate
Printed and bound in the USA

Published in Canada by Doubleday Canada,
a division of Random House of Canada Limited

Visit Random House of Canada Limited's website:
www.randomhouse.ca

BVG 10 9 8 7 6 5 4 3 2 1

For R.W., my first love,
and R.J., my love forever

one

Dear ED (electronic diary),

Happy New Year.

I'm sorry I haven't written lately. I've been crazy busy. Okay, I am so completely lying right now. I haven't done much of anything these past two weeks. Unless you consider staring at my split ends, ignoring my mother, watching my all-time favorite teenage drama, *Minors in Malibu*, and waiting for school to start as doing something.

I so need this winter break to be o-v-e-r.

Surprisingly, not doing much of anything has been emotionally exhausting.

There's no such thing as privacy in my house. Having "alone time" is not an option when the Queen is around. Which is why I haven't logged on ED, my dear electronic diary.

In only 16 hours, 27 minutes, and 45 seconds—not that I'm counting or anything—I'll be back at Cactus High. You know me, ED—I'm not some freak of nature who gets off on the scent of textbooks or sucking up to teachers or anything like that.

I just cannot stand to be under the same roof as my mother, for more than, um, five minutes.

I know, I know. How can this be, right? My mother is, after all, Dr. Bee Bee Berg! The one and only Dr. Bee Bee Berg! Cheers all around!

I'm well aware that my mother's die-hard followers, who plop on their couches every weekday at 5 p.m. to listen to the good old-fashioned relationship wisdom spewing from my mother's mouth during her syndicated talk show, *Queen of Hearts with Dr. Bee Bee Berg*, would cut off their right arm to have the Queen hovering around them 24/7.

The millions of viewers who watch her show religiously would just love, love, LOVE to have Dr. Bee Bee Berg worm her way into their brains by asking them a thousand times a day how they're "feeling" and if they'd like her "advice."

I am NOT one of those people.

Trust me, being interrogated about how you're feeling 24/7 is about as much fun as waking up to a huge whitehead pimple . . . in the center of your nose.

It's been just my luck my mother's talk show happens to be in repeats during my winter break. In television-land, they call this a "hiatus." What it really means is that she's been at home, every single minute of every single day, treating me like one of her television guests— guests who are only too willing and eager to answer personal questions about the most intimate details of their relationships—in front of millions of viewers AND a studio audience. I know, right, ED? How personal is that?

My mother has spent the last two weeks wanting to talk, talk, talk, talk. I keep reminding her that, at home, she's not on television, that no one is watching her, and that I'm not heading to my room to pout because all my best friends are away.

I just want at least a little peace and QUIET!

She should know I am the Sponge. Have I told you, ED, that's what my best friends, Happy and Brooklyn, have always called me? I soak up all my feelings and keep everything inside. You'd literally have to wring my neck and pull out my fingernails one by one to get me to talk about anything personal.

And what's so wrong with that, ED? When did keeping things to yourself and being a private person become such a bad thing? Not everyone in the world needs advice or needs to share every feeling that passes through their head.

Not that I have any major relationship problems I'd need advice about anyway. Not everyone in the world has relationship issues. Take Zen. Zen has never known about my crush on him. Good thing, too, because who knows if I'll ever see him again. Sigh. He has spent the last half year in Australia, being homeschooled by his parents, but I'm sure he's spent most of his time surfing and meeting new friends. Why would he ever want to come back from living like that? I may NEVER see him again. Unlike some people, I don't think that every thought that passes through my head or every feeling in my heart needs to be discussed to death. And really, if I

could just forget about him altogether, I would. I haven't even told Happy or Brooklyn about my crush on him. Speaking of my best friends, I'm heading off to meet them at Gossip Spa. Finally I'll get away from Dr. Bee Bee Berg, who is yelling at me right now from somewhere downstairs—"Are you okay up there? What are you doing? You need advice on what to wear?"
I know, ED, I know. Welcome to my life.

♡

Shoot me now, Apple thought. Put me out of my misery. Just shoot me now!

"You want my advice?" Dr. Bee Bee Berg called out, just as Apple managed to get one foot out the front door. Dr. Bee Bee Berg—*my mother!*—had appeared out of nowhere, and now she was standing with one hand holding the door open so Apple couldn't shut it behind herself.

"I think you should get out of those ripped jeans you've been living in for the past two weeks and put on something a little nicer. Honestly, I'm surprised nothing is growing on those things. You will feel better on the inside if you dress nicely on the outside."

Of course, her mother would say that. Dr. Bee Bee Berg, even when she wasn't on air, was always impeccably groomed. Today she was wearing a white cashmere sweater, white slacks, and open-toed sandals, which featured her French-manicured toes. Every strand of her hair, as always, was perfectly in place.

"Mom, I didn't ask for your advice. And I'm *fifteen*! I think I can dress myself!" Apple responded, trying to remain calm.

Apple would have made it out the door, too, if only she hadn't been wearing her kitten-heeled ankle boots, which had clicked on the marble-tiled floors in the long hallway and had given her away.

Because of the high ceilings, every tiny sound in their house echoed. It was like living in a shower stall or the Grand Canyon.

"Will you at least take my advice and put on something a little warmer? It's pretty chilly out there today," Dr. Bee Bee Berg told her daughter, wrapping her arms around herself and rubbing them for emphasis. "You don't want to get sick before school starts."

Cold outside? That was taking it a bit far, Apple thought. Sure, technically it was January, but it had to be 65 degrees at least.

Apple sighed loudly, stepped back inside the house, and closed the door.

"Excuse me," she said to her mother, stepping around her and opening the hall closet. She was already wearing a thin baby blue sweater over a V-neck T-shirt. But she grabbed a jean jacket from a hanger in the front closet and slid her arms into it.

"Okay now?" she asked her mother. "I'm going to be late for my appointment at Gossip."

Sometimes it was easier just to do what the Queen suggested than to argue with her.

"What are you getting done today at Gossip?" her mother asked. Apple couldn't believe it. Had she not just said, two seconds earlier, that she was going to be late? Her mother always picked the most inappropriate times to want to chat.

"You know," she went on, "when I was a teenager growing up in Buffalo, there was nothing like spas for teenagers around. Not really even for adults. If I had told my mother that I wanted to go for a facial when I was your age, she would have said, 'Aging is a natural process. Don't fight it!' Are you getting a manicure? I always advise women, and men too, that personal upkeep is very important. After all, if you can't even take care of your nails, what does that say about what else you can't take care of? I should really book some spa treatments myself—it's been ages since I've been pampered."

Apple thought, Well, why don't you just *do it* then, instead of telling me about it? But what she said was, "Mom, really, I'm running late. Your questions are making me late. *You're* making me late!" She just couldn't keep the annoyance from dripping off her tongue, thick as honey.

"Apple, all I asked was what you were getting done at Gossip. It's a simple question," her mother answered, sounding perplexed at her daughter's tone. "It would take only two seconds to answer."

"I'm going to get my eyebrows done, okay?" Apple answered, through gritted teeth.

"Okay. Are you meeting Happy and Brooklyn there?" Dr. Bee Bee Berg asked next. "I can drive you, you know. You don't have to walk. I'm more than happy to drive you, if you're running that much behind."

Apple liked to walk. She could walk for hours, taking in the peaceful scenery. She enjoyed the solitude of walking. She enjoyed the *silence*. That's all Apple ever wanted: silence.

And Gossip was only a twenty-minute walk from her home—*if* she could ever get out of the house.

"Yes, Mom. I'm meeting Happy and Brooklyn there. And I *want* to walk. I really have to go now." Apple opened the door for the second time.

"Well, ask them how their vacations went," her mother said. "I know seeing them will cheer you up. I can tell that you've been down ever since school break started, so you must be pretty excited to have them back. I just wish you'd talk to me more about your feelings about it all. You know, five million people would love to talk to me about *their* feelings," Dr. Bee Bee Berg reminded her.

Her mother was unbelievable. She could not, would not, take the hint.

"I know, Mom. You don't have to remind me. I'm well aware of what you do for a living," Apple sighed, adding under her breath, "You never let me forget it." Apple wondered how different her life would have turned out if her mother had been an accountant or a dentist, and not the third most famous relationship talk show host in the country.

"Apple, I'm worried about you. It's not healthy to not talk about your feelings and problems," Dr. Bee Bee Berg told her, for like the six millionth time in the last two weeks.

Apple rolled her eyes.

"Okay, Mom. I'm going now for real," Apple said, and added, "I feel fine. Honestly, there's nothing to talk about. I'm fine."

"Apple, seriously, you want my advice about—"

Apple slammed the door before her mother could finish. She felt a pang of guilt hit her gut. She didn't want to be rude to her mother, but at that moment, she felt she just had to get away or she would start screaming, "Can you please just shut up already? Shut up. Shut up. Shut up!"

Apple raced down the sidewalk, passing the large houses of her guard-gated community, Silver Ranch. Her neck and shoulders were tense, as they always were when she was irritated. She wondered if maybe she should have booked herself a massage instead. She walked by the tree-lined streets and small parks, took in the Spanish-style homes, and tried to calm her breathing and stop thinking about Dr. Bee Bee Berg. Apple had once heard that if you counted to ten while breathing in and out slowly, it would make the lump in your throat go away and calm you down.

Her shoulders started to relax and her thoughts turned away from her mother's questions and the guilt of slamming the door in her face to the excitement of soon seeing her two best friends.

Since Apple was an only child, Happy and Brooklyn were the closest she had to sisters—aside from Crazy Aunt Hazel, that is, but she was a whole other story. Apple couldn't wait to get to Gossip, not only so she could finally get her eyebrows shaped, but also so she could complain to Happy and Brooklyn about Dr. Bee Bee Berg.

"You want my advice, girls?" Apple imagined herself saying, imitating her mother's no-nonsense tone, to her friends as they were getting their treatments. "I think you should stop biting your nails, Brooklyn. And Happy? You want my advice? I think you should stop smiling so much. You'll get lines."

She knew her best friends would laugh, politely, at Apple's impersonation of her mother.

But Apple also knew that, no matter how much Apple complained about her mother, her best friends believed that Dr. Bee Bee Berg was the coolest parent in the world. Nothing Apple could do—no impersonations, no amount of bitching—would ever change that, no matter how hard she tried.

Happy and Brooklyn thought Apple was truly lucky to be the only daughter of the one and only Dr. Bee Bee Berg. They often said how fortunate she was to always have a "professional" around to give her advice for free. And a famous one, too!

Happy's parents, after all, paid Happy's therapist $200 an hour, once a week, to listen to her and try to fix her problems, and her therapist wasn't even on television and hadn't written six advice and self-help books, like Dr. Bee Bee Berg had.

"How's it going, Applesauce?" George, the day gateman, called out as she walked by.

Today even George's friendly question annoyed Apple. And it annoyed Apple that it annoyed her. George was a nice man, and the only person she would let get away with calling her "Applesauce."

She gave George a half-hearted smile.

"I'm good, George. How are you?" she asked.

"Great, Applesauce. I'm just great. How's the Queen of Hearts?" he asked.

"Oh, she's fine," responded Apple. "Just enjoying her time off."

"Well, you tell her to get back to work. It gets quite boring in this booth without having your mother's show to look forward to," George said, pointing to the mini television in his booth, as proud as if he were showing Apple a photograph of his own family.

"I'll let her know. See you later, George," said Apple with a polite smile.

"Later, Applesauce," said George, tipping his hat. "You have yourself a good day."

Apple flashed him another half smile. From the time she had been able to understand words, Apple had realized there would always be questions and "cute" comments about her name. Being named after a fruit kind of did that to your life. In fact, Apple often joked that her first name might as well have been "Conversation" and her last name "Starter," because people were always asking if that was her real name and why in the world would her parents have named her that.

Apple supposed there were worse fruits to be named after. Her mother said she had named her Apple because she thought it was a "delicious"-sounding name. That and she had craved apples when she was pregnant. At least her mother hadn't craved mangos or kiwis. Thank God for small miracles, thought Apple. Brooklyn always tried to make Apple feel better about her name by saying, "Hello? My name is Brooklyn!

Where do you think I was conceived?" And Happy? Happy had no idea why her parents had named her Happy. "Maybe they were happy for that five minutes it took to conceive me," Happy often joked. "Or maybe my mother was just happy to have me finally come out of her."

Apple continued to inhale deeply in through her nose and blow air slowly out of her mouth as she walked along the quiet highway. A golfer drove by in a fancy golf cart and waved at her.

"Nice day, isn't it?" he asked.

Whatever, Apple thought. She raised her hand back in greeting. Why does everyone have to be so friendly all the time here? Why was everyone asking her questions?

two

Fifteen minutes later, Apple arrived at Market Mall, the plaza (even though it was called a "mall") where Gossip was located. She loved having Market Mall and all its high-end stores so close to her home, even if some of the shops were pretty ridiculous. She passed Spa Dogs, an upscale boutique for "pampered pets," which sold dog clothes and organic dog foods and hosted dog fashion shows every month. She looked in the windows of Facial Furnishings, a store dedicated to funky eyewear, and of one of her favorite boutiques, Savvy Girl, which sold clothes from the four M's—Miami, Melrose, Milan, and Manhattan.

Still, Apple swore her brain hadn't stopped ringing from her mother's questions—before she realized that what she was hearing was actual ringing. Her cell phone was going off in her bag, and she hadn't noticed.

Apple stuck her hand in her tote bag, riffling through the keys, lip gloss, gum, old movie tickets, her iPod, her wallet, and the change at the bottom of her purse.

Why did they have to make cell phones so small? Why hadn't she carried a smaller purse?

"I can't find anything in here," Apple moaned under her breath, standing still while still fishing around in her bag, feeling a million items but not her phone. "Where is the damn thing?"

Screw it, Apple thought, as she knelt down on the sidewalk outside a store called Health Nuts. She dumped the contents of her purse out on the ground. It wasn't like there was anything important or valuable in there, and the sidewalks at this plaza were eerily clean—just like all the spotless cars. And everyone's gleaming white teeth in magazine advertisements.

Apple finally found her pink cell phone.

"Hello? Hello?" she asked breathlessly, flipping it open. No answer. Great, Apple thought, throwing her phone back into her bag in disgust. Can anything go right in my life today?

She stayed crouched, hanging her head so her long, super-curly brown hair fell over her face, and covered her eyes with her hands, taking a moment to calm down. Maybe she should go into Health Nuts one of these days and ask about some sort of natural pill for relaxation.

Breathe, Apple, just breathe. It's just a missed phone call. As Brooklyn would say, "Let all your bad energies out. Think only positive thoughts."

"Breathe, Apple, just breathe," she said again.

"Bad day?" a deep voice asked above her.

Apple looked up, surprised. She hadn't realized she had been talking out loud. She felt her face turning pink.

Apple hated how she blushed so easily. What was the point of being a private person if the feelings just seeped out of your skin and made you blush? She had to work on that.

She couldn't help but notice that the guy standing above her, looking directly down at her, was cute—*super* cute. His lips were bee-stung plump, turned upward in a half smile. His eyes were as blue as the ocean. He had the sweetest dimple in his right cheek. *And* he was smiling at her. Apple was mortified. There she was, crouching on the ground outside Health Nuts, muttering to herself, surrounded by an old issue of *Teen Vogue*, crumpled papers, dirty tissues, and old gum packages, like some sort of crazy person. She felt her face turning redder.

"No, um, I just missed a call, that's all. It's not a big deal," Apple answered, frantically starting to shove everything she had dumped out back into her bag. "I couldn't find my freaking phone in this bag. It's like an endless pit leading to nowhere."

"Was it an important call?" the cute guy asked, bending down to talk to Apple at eye level. Apple looked down. She wasn't good at looking people directly in the eye. It made her uncomfortable. The cute guy started helping her pick up the contents of her bag, handing over a package of gum, which Apple grabbed and threw into her purse, along with a package of bobby pins, her wallet, and a lip gloss she had been trying to find for more than a month.

"No. I doubt it. It was probably just one of my friends. I was supposed to meet them, like, twenty minutes ago, and I'm late. They were probably just wondering where I was. Well, I'd better go. I'm late," Apple said, standing up.

"So you've said," the cute guy responded.

It just figured, thought Apple—I get stopped by a super-cute guy when I'm wearing dirty, stretched-out jeans and on my way to get my eyebrows waxed. Why couldn't I have run into him afterward, when I don't look like Oscar the Grouch?

"That's it?" the cute guy asked. "That's all I get?"

What the heck was he talking about? Did he expect a tip or something? Apple realized she hadn't even thanked him for helping her gather her things. She had been rude to her mother, and now she was being rude to a complete stranger who had just helped her and who was being very kind. She was just not herself today. She was in what her Crazy Aunt Hazel always annoyingly called her "Rotten Apple" mood.

"Oh," Apple said. "I'm sorry. Thank you for helping me." She watched the cute guy stand up. He was at least a head taller than her.

"No, seriously," the cute guy continued. "Come on! Is that really all I get from you?"

"What do you mean?" she asked.

"Apple! It's me! Aren't you even going to ask how the last six months of my life was?" the cute guy asked. "Have you lost your mind along with your cell phone and everything else in that deep and endless pit of a bag of yours? You should really think about cleaning that thing out. Apple, it's me! Me!" he insisted. "Come on! You really don't recognize me?"

Apple turned her eyes up and took a proper look at the cute guy's face, finally forcing herself to even look in his eyes.

"Oh . . . my . . . God," she said, blinking her eyes. How had she not noticed? But he looked so completely different. It couldn't be. Could it?

"Zen?" Apple asked, hesitantly.

"Um, hello? Yes, it's me, Zen," he said with a laugh. "We've only been going to school together for ten years now. I know I was gone for half a year, but still . . ."

Apple suddenly found herself feeling light-headed and slightly dizzy. All the shiny cars trying to find parking in the mall, and the people walking around them on the sidewalk eating ice cream cones suddenly seemed to go into slow motion. It was the same feeling she had always had when she walked by Zen in the hallways at school, or when she knew he was sitting near her on the spiral staircase before classes started.

All she could think was, please, dear God, do not let me faint.

"It's only been six months," protested Zen. "Am I that unforgettable? Do I really look that different?"

How could I ever forget you? Apple thought. I've only thought about you every day for two years. I just spent months wondering if I was ever going to see you again. She cleared her throat and fanned her face. She suddenly felt very hot, as if she had just gone for a long jog.

"I can't believe it," Apple said. "You look . . . well . . . you look so different. What happened to your glasses? And your hair! It looks so much longer and blonder. You look . . . you look . . . you look . . . you look so much taller," she gushed. And she thought—this time *only* in her head—and you look like you've been working out! Where did those shoulders come from? Where did those washboard abs come from?

Apple hated herself for stuttering. She hated herself for gushing. She was a stuttering, gushing moron.

Breathe, Apple, just breathe.

"'Different' meaning good? Or 'different' meaning bad?" Zen asked, smiling his dimpled smile.

"'Different' meaning amazing!" Apple heard herself gush again. She knew the words coming out of her mouth made her sound idiotic. She had to tone it down a notch—or five hundred notches. "I mean, you know, you look healthy. Very healthy. That's all I meant. You look really, really healthy. You look very different and really healthy."

I did not just use the word "healthy" four times in one sentence, Apple moaned inwardly. Please tell me I did not.

"I decided to get contact lenses," Zen said, "so maybe that's the 'different.' You can't exactly surf with glasses. And my hair, I know it's a little long, but six months' surfing in the Australia sun does make it lighter, and I guess grow faster or something." He touched his hair. "I guess hanging out with all those surfers got to me or something, because I kind of like it like this."

"Well, you look incredible," Apple told him. What was wrong with her? "I mean, you look incredibly healthy."

"Well, I'll take 'healthy' as a compliment. So how are *you*?" Zen asked. "How was your semester?"

"Fine. Uneventful. Boring. The usual," Apple answered nervously.

Apple found it hard to speak in full sentences to this new Zen. Not that she had ever had an easy time talking to the old Zen, before he became Hot Zen.

Apple could not get over how much he had changed.

She forced herself to turn her eyes away from his face, and stared at the ground, with the same concentration she usually saved for exams or watching *Minors in Malibu*. God forbid Zen could read in her eyes that her Zen crush had, in the last few seconds, just turned into a super-sized Zen Crush. Apple had always thought Zen was sweet-looking and cute. But now? She had to get a grip!

"What are you doing here?" Apple asked, finally. Market Mall was a fun place to hang out with friends at night, but not necessarily on a Sunday afternoon, unless you had an appointment at Gossip.

"I'm just waiting for my mother. She's grabbing some vitamin E oil or something," he said, nodding toward Health Nut.

"Oh," Apple responded.

"Yup," Zen said.

"Well, I guess I better go. I'm late," Apple told him. "You know, to meet Brooklyn and Happy. I'm late. We're meeting at Gossip."

Okay, Apple thought, how pathetic am I? I've used the words "late" and "healthy" way too many times in the last three minutes. Zen will for sure think I'm a nutbar. How could he not?

"I guess I'll see you tomorrow at school then. I'm dreading going back," Zen told her. "Being home-schooled in Australia was so laid back. There wasn't any schedule—I just had to get my work done and send it in. I'm dreading having to go back to a regular schedule."

"Yeah, me too," Apple answered, thinking, *I'm so not dreading going back—especially now that you look the way you do. This was going to make school so much more interesting.*

"Well, it was nice to see you," Zen said, "even if you totally didn't know who I was." Zen laughed.

"I knew! I knew! My mind was just somewhere else," Apple said. "I guess I'll see you tomorrow then."

Apple turned her back to Zen and headed down the sidewalk toward Gossip, fighting the urge to start running.

I'm an idiot, Apple thought. *I'm a stuttering idiot, with a mono-brow. I'm a stuttering mono-browed idiot.*

"Hey, Apple! Wait up a sec!" Apple heard Zen call out. He ran and caught up to her, two storefronts away from Gossip.

Please do not notice my mono-brow, Apple thought, turning around to face her super-sized Zen Crush once again. Was it possible Zen wanted to talk to her longer? Or to ask her something important, like if she wanted to hook up sometime?

"Yeah?" she asked. She could literally hear the gulp in her throat as she swallowed, and wondered if Zen could hear it too.

"You forgot this. It's not exactly what I'm into—I have no use for it," Zen said, holding his arm out toward her, smiling broadly. *Oh, that dimple!*

Apple swore that she could actually feel her heart melting.

"Oh. Thanks very much," she said, taking the *Teen Vogue* from Zen's outreached hand, all the while wishing the ground would open and swallow her up.

"I'm late," she said again, and raced off past the last couple of doors to Gossip. Why was it always so hard to breathe when Zen was around?

three

"There you are!" screeched Happy the moment Apple raced into Gossip Spa. Happy had been standing near the tower of nail polishes by the nail bar just inside the door. "Where have you been? You're, like, a month late! I tried calling you, but you didn't pick up. We had to move our appointments back half an hour! Now come here and give me a hug."

"Me too! I want a hug too!" said Brooklyn. "We missed you!"

"I missed you more than Brooklyn did," Happy said.

"Did not," Brooklyn said.

"Did too!"

Happy and Brooklyn embraced Apple into a bear hug, and Apple instantly felt better about life. She inhaled the scent of Happy's long, straight blond hair, which smelled like peach. Hugging Happy was like coming home to a house full of fresh baking.

"You have no idea how much I missed you guys! I can't believe you both left me alone for two weeks. How could you guys do that to me?" Apple asked her friends as they pulled apart. "Take a guess how many times the Queen of Hearts asked me if I wanted her advice. Come on, take a guess!"

"Fifty!" Brooklyn said.

"Nope. Guess again," Apple said.

"Two hundred and fifty," Happy said, as if they were at an auction.

"No, I stopped paying attention after the 285th time," Apple told them.

"I promise we will never do it again," Happy said, "right, Brooklyn? We will never leave sweet Apple alone with her mother for two weeks ever again. Next time, *you* go on vacation with my family, and *I'll* stay at home with Dr. Bee Bee Berg."

"Thank you!" Apple said. "That would be fantastic."

"Right. *You* try spending two weeks with Sailor, and you might think twice about just how painful it is to spend it with your mother," Happy said. "I'll take your mother over my sister any day."

Happy had a real love/hate relationship with her older sister. Sometimes their fights got so out of control that they turned physical. But just as often they hung out together, being only two years apart in age, and they always shared the same clothes.

"Well, *I* had a relaxing holiday," Brooklyn said. "I did sunrise yoga classes on the beach every morning at 6 a.m., and they were truly inspirational."

Happy and Apple exchanged doubtful looks. How

could anything be inspirational at that ungodly hour?

"So what do you think?" Happy asked. "Should I get the slut-red nail polish today, or go for candy-floss pink?" She held two different nail-polish bottles out for Apple to look at.

"I don't know. They're both nice," Apple said. As Happy contemplated the two colors, Apple couldn't help but stare at her.

"Happy," she finally said, "what are you wearing? You *do* realize it's just Sunday afternoon, right? Do you ever not look good?" Happy had the kind of thick, blond hair that celebrities paid a small fortune to fly their hair stylists in to maintain, along with big blue eyes, a perfect ski-slope nose, and high cheekbones. Now, thanks to two weeks in Mexico, she was perfectly bronzed too. And, as always, she was dressed as if she was heading to the MTV Music Awards. Today it was skin-tight black jeans under knee-high black leather boots, and a lacy, almost see-through top.

"No, it's impossible for Happy to ever look bad," Brooklyn said. "You should know that by now. Even Happy's worst-looking days are better than my best-looking ones," she moaned. Brooklyn was wearing her usual sort of getup—low-waisted yoga pants and a long-sleeved yoga shirt with the words "hugs make the world go round" written across the chest.

"You guys are too nice!" Happy said. "I don't know why I need therapy when I have you guys to make me feel so good all the time."

"Yeah, well there's a reason they call you 'the Onion' at school," Brooklyn said.

"Oh, God, stop it!" Happy moaned, shaking her head. "I hate that."

It was true that all their classmates called Happy "the Onion" behind her back, and sometimes even to her face. It was because she was so beautiful that, when you looked at her, you wanted to cry. "Mind you, at least I'm not called the Noodle," Happy said, looking at Brooklyn, who could bend her body like a boiled noodle. Brooklyn was tall, lean, limber, and willowy, like a ballerina. "I'd rather be called the Onion than the Noodle, wouldn't you, Apple?"

"Um, I'd rather be called neither," Apple said.

"Apple? Your skin looks amazing! You look like you just had an oxygen facial recently or something. Did you?" Happy asked.

"No! I just got here," said Apple. "Plus I'd never come to Gossip without you guys. It's our thing, right?"

Apple, Happy, and Brooklyn came to Gossip Spa on a pretty regular basis. They came to celebrate special occasions, like their birthdays or Valentine's Day, and always on the last day of school break, before school started up again. They called it "back-to-school" pampering.

"I don't know, Apple," Happy said. "Your skin looks all flushed. You're glowing! You're not pregnant, are you?"

"Happy!" Apple said, laughing. The things that came out of her mouth, Apple thought. It was one of the reasons she loved Happy so much: she always kept Apple on her toes. Happy didn't know how to edit her own words.

"You're not in love, are you?" asked Brooklyn, clapping her hands like a little child who had just been handed a balloon. "You look like you're in love! Are you in love?"

"God, you guys. No, I'm not in love. No, I'm not pregnant. I've never even had a boyfriend, as you two know perfectly well," Apple said. But maybe I will this semester, she thought. Zen smiled at me, after all.

"Not that she'd tell you anyway, Happy. She's the Sponge," said Brooklyn, trying out a purple hue on her big toe.

"Oh, the Sponge would tell us *big* news," Happy said to Brooklyn, pretending Apple wasn't standing right beside them. "One day, the Sponge is going to explode, and we're going to know all her secrets. No one can keep everything inside for that long without blowing up."

"Guys, I'm *not* pregnant. I'm *not* in love. I just raced over here," Apple insisted. "I was practically running. My face is flushed because my mother made me late with her stream of never-ending questions on the way out the door. That's why. I swear!"

"Okay, moving on," said Happy. "So you're getting the 'Hello Gorgeous' today?" she asked Apple.

The Hello Gorgeous was one of the most popular treatments at Gossip. It promised to shape your eyebrows so perfectly that you'd be ready for the pages of a magazine.

"Hey, Apple! You have to hear all about Happy's new man," Brooklyn suddenly said, looking up from her feet.

"He was just a fling, Brooklyn," said Happy, adding, "a super-hot fling. That's what my parents get for forcing me to go to Mexico with them and Sailor. I swear, my parents never want to spend any time with us, and then when we have two weeks off, that's the time they decide they want to 'get to know' us. Not that they really even did that. Sailor and I barely saw them the entire vacation. They had their own room and we had ours. Sailor and I fought the entire time. One night, Sailor—"

"Happy!" Apple said. "Enough about Sailor! Tell me about the fling!"

"He was a lifeguard," Happy said, beaming. "Sailor was so jealous! It was totally worth it, just to see the envy dripping from Sailor that I had found a guy and she hadn't. It was, like, the happiest days of my life."

"Okay, *you* had a fling with a lifeguard and all *I* did was watch reruns of *Minors in Malibu* for two weeks and stare at my split ends," Apple moaned.

"Well, there's not much to tell, though. Let's just say I have a whole new appreciation for lifeguards." Happy laughed.

Apple had a million questions for Happy, but before she could ask any of them, Natalie, the owner of Gossip, sauntered over to them.

Natalie was twenty-five and was the coolest adult Apple had ever met. She was always dressed like she was about to walk down a red carpet at a movie premiere. She had had features written about her in all the local newspapers and magazines. And, unlike Apple's mother, she never shelled out unwanted advice—she only shelled it out when asked. But she always treated her clients like friends, and you could tell her anything. Not that Apple ever did.

"Hey, you guys! It's so nice to see you. It's been way too long! And you all look phenomenal!" Natalie said, giving them each a hug.

That was the other thing about Natalie. She was always so free with compliments. "Are you all ready for your treatments?" Natalie asked. "Brooklyn, you're getting your legs waxed, right? Kendra is waiting for you in the back."

"In the torture room, right?" Brooklyn asked with a shudder.

"You got it," said Natalie.

"See you guys soon," Brooklyn said, "I may be a while. My leg hair is so long you could practically braid it. And I hate when people in my yoga classes stare at my hairy legs. I'm not *that* much of a tree-hugger."

"Nice, Brooklyn," Happy said, and they all laughed. Brooklyn gave them a peace sign and headed to the back.

"And Apple, you're getting the Hello Gorgeous, right?" said Natalie. "Michele is waiting for you at the eyebrow bar. And Happy, you can head over to the nail bar with Jessica," she directed.

"Do you think maybe Jessica can do my nails at the eyebrow bar? I need to catch up with Apple," Happy asked Natalie.

"Yes, Happy has to tell me about her new lifeguard boyfriend!" added Apple.

"Oooh, a lifeguard!" said Natalie. "That's my greatest fantasy. Too bad I have another client in the back waiting for me. I'll have to hear all about this the next time you guys are here, which I hope will be soon. And, yes, Happy, Jessica can do your nails next to Apple while she gets her brows done. Be nice to Jessica—she's new here. See you guys soon," said Natalie, heading off to attend to her client, who looked like a Paris Hilton wannabe and who was bragging to the receptionist about her new nose.

"Man, Paris-ites," Happy moaned. "Can't live with them, can't live without them. I blame that awful show on them multiplying like fleas."

"*The Queen of Hearts*?" Apple asked, only half joking.

"No, that one you loved that was canceled after, like, two shows," Happy responded.

Apple knew Happy was talking about a docu-soap that had recently put their city on the map, but not in a good way. The show had featured seven upper-class women who lived in the area and who had discussed their marriages, cheating, and what it was like to be "trophy wives." All the women dressed—and acted—twenty years younger than they actually were. It was the worst of reality shows, but in a fascinating way.

"Why did you hate that show and not my mother's show?" Apple asked. "I mean, they basically discussed relationship issues too, just not in the same way."

"Because at least your mother's show is real! And your mother helps them at the end," Happy said. "And she doesn't let anything get by her. She knows when someone is lying to her, and she gets it out of them. Now *that* is fascinating to watch!"

"Well, I guess it's more real than that girl's chest and nose, anyway," laughed Apple, nodding toward the girl at the reception desk. "How old do you think she is? Seventeen?"

"If even," Happy answered. "Come on, Oscar. Let's get your brows done."

four

Dear ED,

What a day! First I ran into Zen. He's back! And, oh my God, was I a bumbling idiot. I don't think there has ever been a more flustered human in the world. I swear, and I would only admit this to you, ED, I'm going to start taking pointers from my mother's book, because I cannot be like that in front of Zen again. Ever! I'm going on a mission, I tell you. I'm going to call it Plan Z. (Short for Plan Zen, if you didn't get it.) I also went to Gossip and was so happy to see Brooklyn and Happy. Happy had a fling with a lifeguard! He was seventeen years old and she didn't even ask for his phone number or e-mail address when she left. She didn't even know his last name! And she would only tell me the details of her fling if I gave her something in return. And you're not going to believe what she has asked me to do! And because I was still so flustered from running into Zen, I actually agreed to do it! But I'll get into that soon enough. At least my mother is starting work again tomorrow. The show has been in reruns, so now she can go back to meddling in other people's lives. Anyway, back to my promise to Happy in order for Happy to give me the details of her fling. Happy is so addicted to *Queen of Hearts with Dr. Bee Bee Berg* (even more addicted than I am to *Minors in Malibu*!), so not only does Happy want me to find out what my mother's upcoming shows are, so she can be in the know before everyone else—which is painful enough—but she also wants to know how she can get on the show! Happy wants to be a guest on my mother's show! I mean, I know Happy has always wanted to be an actress and she thinks that getting on my mother's show as a guest will be the place she gets "discovered." I told her just to go to my mother's website, where people write in for advice, but Happy actually wants to be on the show, in front of the audience and everything! What could I do? I mean, she is my best friend and I promised. I wasn't thinking clearly! But she also promised me this fabulous pair of jeans that she has that I've always adored. So I guess I have to do it—at least for the jeans! (Once I get my Plan Z into action, and he sees me in them, they'll be an added bonus!) I really, really need those jeans. And now I have to get downstairs for "family dinner." Which is such a joke. I mean, my parents don't really seem to spend any time together at all. And to top it off, Crazy Aunt Hazel is here. All I'll say about her is that she is a walking, talking memo reminding me how I DO NOT want my life to end up. Once again, welcome to my life, ED.

"I just can't believe he broke up with me," Apple heard her aunt Hazel moan loudly as she walked into the large open kitchen. "Everything seemed to be going fine. And then, poof, out of the blue he decides he needs 'space.' Space! Can you believe that? Why would he want space from me? I was the ideal girlfriend. I did everything for him! I was always there for him. Always. I worked my entire schedule around him!"

Apple knew that Crazy Aunt Hazel was grousing about her latest dating disaster. She was always having a major crisis about a man, and Apple's mother was always giving her advice, which Aunt Hazel always ignored.

"Maybe that was the problem," her mother responded, in full Dr. Bee Bee Berg mode.

Apple sat down at the kitchen table, across from her aunt, resting her feet on another chair. Her mother was putting out dinner plates on the table, which was already full of cartons of takeout Chinese food. Dr. Bee Bee Berg could solve all matters of the heart, but she couldn't even manage to make scrambled eggs or to microwave frozen peas.

"So Rupert broke up with you?" Apple asked her aunt, who had started, literally, to pound her head on the table. Her hair was a disaster, as if she had just been caught in a tornado. Her shirt was even on inside out.

"His name was Roger," Crazy Aunt Hazel huffed, hiding her face in her hands. It looked like she still had on her makeup from the night before.

Roger, that's it! Apple thought. *I knew it started with an R.*

It was hard for Apple to keep track of all the men who moved in and out of Aunt Hazel's life like it had a revolving door. The taste in a piece of chewing gum lasted longer than Aunt Hazel's relationships. And all Aunt Hazel wanted was to fall in love, get married, and have babies.

"I didn't even hear you come in, sweetie," Apple's mother said. "So did you have fun with the girls?"

"Yes," Apple answered, crossing her legs on the chair.

"What's up with your friends?"

"Not much," Apple answered, trying to sound friendly but not so friendly as to invite more questions.

"Come on. What did you guys talk about?" her mother pressed.

There was no way Apple was going to tell her mother about Happy's lifeguard. That was Happy's life and Happy's business. And Apple didn't think Crazy Aunt Hazel would want to hear about the fling either, given that a fifteen-year-old was probably getting more action than she was.

"I don't remember," Apple said.

"Well, you look good. Your eyebrows look all cleaned up," her mother said. "They're perfect!"

"Hello? We were talking about *me*," Crazy Aunt Hazel interrupted, throwing up her arms. Apple noticed there was a hole in her shirt under her armpit. She really was a mess. "Apple," she said, "one day you will learn that it's impossible to find a good man. They all disguise their real personalities. They seem really nice and kind at first, and they treat you like a goddess. Then, after three weeks of bliss, the mask comes off. The mask *always* comes off. And you realize that they are commitment-phobic and that they'll never say 'I love you,' and then they'll tell you that they never promised you anything and that they need space," Crazy Aunt Hazel ranted. She tilted her head back in despair. "He was probably cheating on me."

Apple knew what was coming. One did not complain to Dr. Bee Bee Berg about a relationship gone sour without getting a rant in return. It amazed Apple that, after all these years, her aunt still hadn't learned this.

"Hazel! That's just not true," her mother responded, just as Apple knew she would. "You can't make sweeping generalizations like that about men. Not every man cheats. Many men do say 'I love you.' Not every man needs space. You just haven't met the right man for you—your time will come. Patience is a virtue. Men are like dogs: they smell desperation. If you act positive, then positive things will come your way."

It annoyed Apple that her mother was always optimistic about love. She did kind of have to be, though. After all, it was her job. Although Apple couldn't help but think that it would be kind of cool if one day her mother just went postal on *The Queen of Hearts* and shouted out to one of her guests, "Just give up on love, you pathetic loser!" Now *that* would be a show worth watching, Apple thought. She grabbed an egg roll and filled her plate with beef and broccoli.

"That's easy for you to say," moaned Aunt Hazel, reaching into a carton of fried rice and taking it out with her hands.

"Hazel! Can you at least use a fork?" her mother reprimanded her younger sister.

After Hazel swallowed, she placed her head on the table as if she was going to take a nap. But she continued to speak. "You are already married. You have a job you love. You have a child. You have a home. You're famous. Your life is just peachy keen. It's the same way as it's easy for rich people to say that money doesn't buy happiness, because they *have* money. It's easy for people who are married to say, 'You'll find someone.'"

"You want to know what I think?" Apple's mother asked. "I think you need to keep up your energy. Here, have some spare ribs."

"NO!" Aunt Hazel said forcefully. "I don't want your advice. I don't want spare ribs. I just want to moan. Can you just listen to me? Can't I just moan?"

"No, you can't. And I'm going to give my advice to you anyway. It's what I wrote in my book *Advice: It's Easier to Give Than to Take*," her mother began.

"Yes, we know all about your best-selling book," Aunt Hazel said, rolling her eyes at Apple. "Remember, Bee Bee? You gave me one when it was published, another for my birthday, another for Valentine's Day, another for Christmas, and another when it went into reprints. I must own five copies of each of your books!"

"And have you read any of them?" Apple's mother demanded, hands on her hips.

"No," said Aunt Hazel, somewhat sheepishly. "I don't like to read."

Apple couldn't help but laugh. Dr. Bee Bee Berg, along with being the host of her popular talk show, had also written six best-selling self-help books. Apple was amazed that so many people bought them. If that were me, Apple thought, you'd bet I'd order them online. There would be no way I'd walk up to someone at a bookstore and let them see that I was buying a book by the Queen of Hearts, even if it was on every best-seller list.

"Well, you will find someone when you stop looking so hard," Apple's mother told Hazel.

"Here we go again," Aunt Hazel said. She sounded remarkably like Apple had earlier that day. Apple realized that, at this moment, she sympathized with her aunt. They both knew what it was like to get unwanted advice all the time, yet it seemed as if Aunt Hazel, unlike Apple, could not stop herself from moaning to Apple's mother all the time about her personal problems. Crazy Aunt Hazel constantly complained about her sister's unwanted advice, but she still called her a thousand times a day telling her about her pathetic love life. What did she expect?

"Do you really think you're the only one out there having a hard time meeting someone special or being in a healthy relationship?" Apple's mother continued. "You should watch my show more often."

"Do *not* compare me to those nut jobs on your show," Aunt Hazel demanded.

"Amen to that," Apple added quietly.

"I can't believe I'm related to you two," Dr. Bee Bee Berg said. "Do you know that, right now, I have about eight hundred e-mails from my viewers asking me for my advice on love problems? Are you telling me that they are all nut jobs? I don't think they are."

"Can we just eat without all the drama?" Apple asked. She was sick of talking and hearing about relationships and about all the people in the world who had relationship problems and needed advice. If her mother and Crazy Aunt Hazel kept talking like this, it wouldn't be long before one of them asked *her* if she had a love interest or any issues with a guy.

"Doug! Doug! Dinner is on the table! We're all here and waiting for you! In fact, we've already started without you," Apple's mother yelled out to her father, who was somewhere in the house. She turned back to her sister.

"Relationships are about compromise," Bee said.

"Oh, please, let this stop! Leave me alone," moaned Aunt Hazel.

"Fine then, I will," said Bee Bee. "But you know I'm right."

"Do you really believe that anyway, Apple? Is that what you do with your boyfriends? Do you compromise?" her aunt asked, saying the word "compromise" as if it was a dirty word.

Dr. Bee Bee Berg turned to Apple, suddenly looking very interested.

"Apple, tell me, is there any boy in your school that I should know about?" her mother said. "Is Hazel right? Is there someone? I know there must be some guy you're interested in. When I was fifteen, I had a whole bunch of boyfriends—it was such an exciting time. Now is the time, Apple, to enjoy male relationships, because they're not nearly as complicated as they will be when you get older. Look at what Hazel goes through."

"Thanks, Bee Bee!" Hazel said, sarcastically.

"No, Mom," Apple said, shooting her aunt an evil look. "There is no one I'm interested in. If we must talk about relationships, let's get back to Aunt Hazel?" Her aunt shot an evil grin back at her.

"Oh, come on! I know you're lying to me. A mother can tell these things. There must be someone you are interested in. What about that boy Hopper in your class? *He's* nice-looking!" her mother said.

"He's also a bit of an ass," Apple responded.

"Language please, Apple," her mother said, disapprovingly. "It's not feminine to talk trashy."

"Well, you asked . . . ," said Apple.

"I know you're keeping something from me, Apple, and I know it will eventually come out. The truth always does." Apple feared her mother really might know what was going on in her head. Her mother's intuition when it came to matters of the heart was amazing, and quite frankly scary sometimes. She could, for example, tell exactly when one of her guests on *Queen of Hearts* was going to cry—she always managed to hand them a tissue moments before the waterworks began. Did her mother know Apple harbored a secret crush on Zen and that she spent hours daydreaming about him? Was it possible that her mother could see something in her eyes?

"Mom, please," Apple begged. "I think I ate too quickly. My stomach hurts."

"Or maybe your stomach hurts because you like someone," her mother said in a singsong voice.

"God, Bee Bee, can you ever stop interrogating anyone for even a second?" asked Aunt Hazel. "If Apple says she's not interested in anyone, she's not interested. Just leave her alone! And that goes for me too."

"Thanks, Aunt Hazel!" Apple said a bit quietly.

Just then, Apple's father walked into the kitchen, wearing his typical Sunday golf ensemble—a checkered pair of pants and a pink shirt.

Apple thought the world of her father, who was a corporate lawyer, and very kind and quiet. Apple knew she took after him way more than she did her mother. Her father understood the need for privacy, which Apple figured was why he spent most of his time at home behind closed doors in his study. He rarely asked Apple about herself. And that was just fine by Apple.

"Well, this is nice," her father said. "Dinner for just the family. Even though you started without me. What's the special occasion?"

It was true that Apple's family rarely sat down for dinner together. Her mother was always working and rarely got home before 10 p.m. She always had to prepare for the next day's show, after the afternoon's live show, and so she ate dinner most nights at her office at the studio, with the staff of producers, camera people, and directors who worked on *Queen of Hearts*. Dr. Bee Bee Berg was also a much-sought-after public speaker, and it seemed that she was invited to at least one glittery charity event every weekend.

"I just thought that because Apple's winter break is over we should all have one nice meal together," her mother said. "And, of course, *Queen of Hearts* starts again tomorrow, and I'll start working late again and won't be here to prepare dinner."

"You mean *pick up* dinner," Apple said.

"Apple, be nice to your mother," said her father, bending to give Apple a kiss on the head before taking his seat at the table. "Let's just enjoy this family time while we can. It happens so rarely. If it weren't for the photos I have at work, and flipping to *Queen of Hearts* once in a while, and seeing my wife's face plastered in newspapers and magazines, I would probably forget what you look like, Bee Bee. Please pass the egg rolls. And for this one dinner, let's not talk about work, shall we? Just this one time, let's not let the questions 'How is that working for you' or 'Is there anything you want to talk about' into the conversation at all. Tonight I want to have dinner with my wife, not with the Queen of Hearts, and with my perfect daughter, Apple. And, of course, with you, Hazel. You *are* part of our family, whether we like it or not," he joked.

Apple's father was a simple, uncomplicated man. All it took for him to be happy was a meal with his family. No muss, no fuss.

"Thanks. You are too good to me," Aunt Hazel said sarcastically. "Pass me the hot and sour soup, please."

"And pass me some of those spicy noodles, honey," Apple's father asked her mother.

"So what did you do today, Dad?" Apple asked, even though she knew the answer.

"Golf, of course," he answered.

"Run into Alice Cooper?" she asked.

"Not yet. But one day—I know it will happen," he said.

It had become a running joke between Apple and her father that some day he would run into the shock rocker, who was, apparently, an avid golfer and who owned a home nearby.

"Here are your noodles," Apple's mother said. "But there's just a little something you should know about this quiet family dinner, Doug."

"Let me guess. You forgot to order those fried wontons I love?" her dad asked, scanning the cartons on the table. "Wait . . . there's an extra place setting on the table. Why, Bee Bee?"

"Well, there will be one more person joining us. But he's a part of our family, sort of," she answered, speaking quickly and avoiding her husband's eye.

As if a director had yelled "action," at that moment they all heard the front door open then slam shut.

"Hello! Hello! Guy's here! Guy hasn't missed dinner, has he? Sorry Guy's late. Guy had a wardrobe malfunction! Meaning, Guy just *couldn't* pick out what to wear."

That was Guy, her mother's long-time assistant on *Queen of Hearts*. He had his own key to their house, because, like Aunt Hazel, he spent a lot of time there. Guy walked—rather, strutted—into the kitchen as if he was a model on a runway, wearing a bright orange scarf around his neck and what looked like bowling shoes.

Only Guy could get away with an outfit like that, Apple thought with admiration.

"Bee Bee!" her father said angrily. "I thought this was a family night! Sorry, Guy, but I'm a little taken aback to see you here."

Apple was stunned at his reaction to Guy's entrance. Her father was usually so gracious. And it wasn't like this never happened. Her mother spent more time, and more dinners, with Guy than with her husband.

Guy, however, didn't seem bothered. "Hey, sweet Apple. And Hazel," he said, kissing each of their hands in greeting before turning to Bee Bee.

"There she is! The Queen of Hearts looking her very best. How excited are we for tomorrow? Guy is very excited!" he said, bending down to peck her on each cheek. "And no offense taken, Doug. I know you love Guy, even if you pretend you don't. How could you *not* love him?"

That was the other thing about Guy. He *always* talked about himself in the third person.

"Guy, we're just in the middle of dinner. Any chance you can come back in a couple of hours?" Apple's father asked in all seriousness. "Or wait for Bee Bee in her office? Maybe you could get started on work, while we finish our dinner. We could make you a plate to take upstairs with you if you're hungry."

Apple looked down at her plate. She did not like confrontation—which was why she was never entirely comfortable watching her mother's show.

"Honey," Apple's mother said calmly, then pointed to his place setting at the head of the table. "I invited him! Not only is he a part of this family, but the show starts tomorrow and we have to get organized. Guy, sit down. There's plenty of food for everyone, especially my number one man, who makes my work life come together so effortlessly."

Apple glanced at her father, who looked less than thrilled at the compliments her mother was throwing out to Guy. Apple thought he even looked hurt.

"There's no rest for the wicked," Guy said, sitting down at the table. He was holding onto a large folder. "And Guy *loves* to be wicked!"

"Are those our shows for the next few weeks?" Apple's mother asked, snatching the folder from Guy's hand. "I can't wait to start solving people's problems. Apparently, no one around *here* needs my help." She looked pointedly at Apple and Hazel.

"Do you want to start going over them now?" Guy asked. "We can eat and work at the same time. This promises to be the best season yet! You should *see* the guests Guy has lined up."

"You know what?" Aunt Hazel said, getting up from the table. "I'm really not in the mood to listen to romantic problems right now. So, Apple, am I picking you up tomorrow to take you to school?"

Hazel was a salesperson in the lingerie department at a high-end department store and never started work before 10 a.m. And since Apple's parents left for work early, and she didn't have an older sister like Happy did to drive her to school, Crazy Aunt Hazel was often her personal chauffeur. In exchange for practically living at their house and eating all their food,

Aunt Hazel helped take care of Apple. It had been like this Apple's whole life.

"Yes, please," Apple answered. "Same time as always, okay?"

"Same time," said Aunt Hazel. She headed to the fridge and grabbed a carton of cookie dough ice cream on her way out, saying, "I'm taking this. Later!" She slammed the door behind her.

"What is up her ass?" Guy asked, looking at Apple's mother. "Oh, sorry, Apple. Excuse my language. Did she by any chance get dumped *again*?"

"Oh, can you tell?" asked Bee Bee. "At least there is one plus about being dumped—you can eat cookie dough ice cream without feeling guilty."

"Guy hears that, sister," Guy said, slapping his left thigh, then sighing dramatically. "Guy's thighs have not been the same since Brad left him. I really should start hitting the gym again."

Apple liked Guy, though she would never admit to her mother that she thought he was pretty cool and good for a laugh. She felt torn, though, because her dad obviously was upset with Guy being there tonight. She didn't want her dad to feel like a second fiddle.

"It's just Hazel being Hazel," Apple's mother sighed. "Of course she got dumped again because she never listens to me. It's like I wrote in my book—"

"You know what?" Apple's father said suddenly, getting up from the table. "I've suddenly lost my appetite too."

"Honey!" her mother said. "Don't be like that."

"Be like what?" he responded. "You clearly have to get to work this instant. You clearly are not interested in having a conversation that doesn't center on your show. You clearly are not interested in having dinner with *me*."

"You know how important my show is, honey. It's my life!" her mother said. "We've worked so hard to get to this point. And you know what they say—you're only as good as your last show."

"Don't 'honey' me. You know how supportive I am and always have been. But when you actually want to have dinner with me, let me know," he said, and walked out of the kitchen.

Apple guessed her father was heading up to his study to watch the Golf Channel. She thought her mother should go after him, but she knew that would never happen. The show *always* came first. It seemed as though her mother was married to her show first, and to Apple's dad second.

Wasn't it Bee Bee who, just moments ago, told Crazy Aunt Hazel that relationships were based on compromise? Would it have killed her mother to spend a half hour eating with her father before getting to work? Why couldn't Bee Bee see that she wasn't paying as much attention to her *own* relationship as she was to those of perfect strangers?

Apple wanted to leave the kitchen too, excusing herself by saying that Guy and her mother should really get to work and that she didn't want to be in the way. She wanted to stand by her father. He had a point— Apple's mother really didn't want to have dinner with her, either, it seemed.

But there was that promise to Happy that she'd find out what the upcoming *Queen of Hearts with Dr. Bee Bee Berg* topics were going to be. And Apple really wanted those jeans.

"So what exactly is in the folder?" she asked Guy.

"Well, my dear, like Guy just told your mother, it's all the information for the upcoming shows, of course!"

"Let's hear them," her mother said, wiping her face delicately with a napkin. "I'm ready! I'm too excited to eat any more now."

"Okay, this week we have 'Torn between Two Lovers,' 'Commitment-phobic,' 'Should We Get Married?' 'Spouses Who Act Like Children,' 'Men Who Mooch Off Their Wives,' and my favorite, 'Sperm Bandits.'"

"What's a sperm bandit?" Apple asked, apprehensively. She wasn't sure she really wanted to know.

"It's a woman who will lie to her husband or boyfriend about being on the pill so she can secretly get pregnant," Guy answered.

"Oooh, fascinating!" Dr. Bee Bee Berg said gleefully.

"Where do you *find* these people?" Apple asked, genuinely amazed.

"Oh, *Guy* can find them," Guy said. "Guy can find *anybody.*"

"So, you're the one who agrees to the people who get on the show?" Apple pressed, remembering her promise to Happy. Apple had stopped paying attention to how the show came together at about the same time she had stopped going with her mother to the studio, eight years ago. In recent years she had just wanted to forget what her mother did altogether.

"Yup. Guy looks at *all* the e-mails, and sometimes we find real gems in what people suggest for show ideas. It's not that hard, really," he said.

"That's it?" Apple asked.

"That's it," Guy said.

"Who cares how he finds them?" Apple's mother interrupted. "These are real issues that real people have, and we're going to help them." She was in full-on Dr. Bee Bee Berg mode. "We're going to give them the very best advice we can give, while offering viewers must-watch television."

"Right on, sister!" Guy said, actually giving Apple's mother a high five.

Apple took that as a sign that it was definitely time to leave the kitchen. She could not put up with the high fives. Plus she had the show list for Happy and knew how to get on *Queen of Hearts*. All Happy would need to do is think of a good show topic and e-mail it to her mother's website. Apple's end of the bargain was done. She imagined herself in those hot jeans.

"Well, I'm going upstairs to my room now," Apple said. "I'm tired."

"Are you sure? You don't want any dessert? Is there something wrong?" her mother asked automatically, but Apple knew she wasn't paying attention anymore, at least not to her.

"No, I'm fine. Just full," Apple said.

"Well, Guy, I guess we should head to my office." Bee Bee and Guy pushed back their chairs at the same time and headed for the stairs, as if Apple were no longer in the room.

"Our viewers' questions are piling up too, and we need to start answering them. I swear, in the two weeks you've been gone, almost a thousand people have sent e-mails. We have so much to do . . ." Her mother's voice trailed off as they walked away.

Apple decided to stay and clear the table. Her mother would probably spend hours working, and if Apple didn't do it, no one would.

Apple knew that Guy was the one who answered the majority of the viewers who sent e-mails to the *Queen of Hearts* website for advice. When he wasn't at the studio with her mother, Guy spent hours alone in her home office, typing out replies to lovelorn viewers. Guy and Dr. Bee Bee Berg had worked together for so long, they could finish each other's sentences. It was almost like they shared the same brain. Not that Apple would ever tell *that* to anyone, not even Happy or Brooklyn. When it came to keeping secrets, Apple also kept her mother's, at least when it came to things that could harm her mother's reputation as the Queen of Hearts. Apple was the Sponge.

five

Dear ED,

Okay, I'll admit it. I'm nervous. And extremely tired. I spent most of the night—gulp—reading one of my mom's advice books. I hardly slept at all last night. I'm heading off to school now, so this is going to have to be a quickie. I get to see my Zen Crush! My hair, at least, is kind of having a good day. It's still boingy—how did I get Aunt Hazel's crazy hair and not my mother's nice, sleek hair? So not fair!—but at least it's not puffy. I can't say so much for my father—the having a good night part—either. I heard him snoring in the spare bedroom last night, which means my parents are not even sleeping in the same room now! And that spare bed is so uncomfortable it makes camping in a tent on a bed of rocks seem like staying at a five-star hotel. I just wish my mother would treat him a bit better. He's a good guy and has always stood by her. Why can't she just see that he's in pain and that his not even wanting to sleep in the same room as her is not a good thing? Unlike me, my father actually wants to spend time with my workaholic mother. I don't get it. But at least I got some advice from my mother's book. Not like I'd ever tell her I read her book. And especially not like I'd ever admit to her that maybe I do need some advice. No, I don't need "advice." I just need some pointers. That's right. I'm going to rename what I need "pointers." I just need a few on as how to get my Zen Crush to turn into a Zen Relationship. According to the book, my first job is simply to talk to him. My mother calls this "baby steps," one of those catchphrases she uses all too often, in my opinion. Then, once I talk to him, we can start having deeper conversations, which, according to my mother, should eventually lead me to asking him if he'd like to do something together, like join me for a movie. I can't believe my mother has made such a successful career out of these "baby steps." But if I'm going to start this new semester on the right foot, I'm going to have to put Plan Z (Plan Zen) into action. First step? Just talk to him without stuttering. I'll kill you, ED, if you ever let it slip that I'm following Dr. Bee Bee Berg's advice—I mean POINTERS. I will deny everything. I swear. Oh, crap, Crazy Aunt Hazel is honking outside. I've got to run. Baby steps . . . baby steps . . .

♡

Okay, my first goal, thought Apple as she headed toward the spiral staircase, where she and all her friends hung out, will be to talk to Zen casually, not to stutter, and not drop anything. And maybe to look him in the eyes. Baby steps, thought Apple, baby steps. All I need to do is ask him about something he's doing. That's it. How hard could that be?

She noticed that Happy, along with Hopper, Cooper, Clover, North, and a few other classmates, was already lounging on the stairs, which were right in the center of the foyer. There were other staircases in other parts of the school for getting between floors, but this middle staircase was where students who wanted to see and be seen hung out.

At first Apple couldn't see any sign of Zen, but then her heart skipped a beat: Hopper leaned back laughing, and let Zen's blond head poke out from behind, smiling that oh-so-adorable smile, with that oh-so-adorable dimple that made Apple blush immediately.

Apple was suddenly terrified, and thought about sneaking away. No, she thought, you *are* doing this. You did not stay up half the night wasting your time reading your mother's book for the first time for nothing.

"Hey, Apple!" Happy said, patting the space on the stair next to her. "Come sit beside me." Apple had no choice now.

"Where's Brooklyn?" Apple asked, nodding hellos to her fellow classmates, trying to stay relaxed.

"Oh, she's somewhere in one of the hallways doing some yoga, she's so stressed over the Helicopter. And you think *your* mother is bad," Happy said. It was true. Brooklyn's mother was the complete opposite of her daughter, whose sole mission in life was to spend a year

51

upon graduation at an ashram, studying with a guru. They called Brooklyn's mother "the Helicopter" because she was always hovering around her daughter, making demands. She was as high-stressed as Brooklyn was laid back. She always needed to know what Brooklyn was up to, every minute of every day.

"Well, I'd say it's a toss-up," Apple said. "Oh, there she is," she added, her eyes resting on Brooklyn, who was lying in the middle of the floor as classmates literally walked over her body. "Oh my God, Happy. What is she doing?"

Brooklyn had just gotten up and folded herself into a back bend.

"God, it's amazing that girl doesn't have a boyfriend. What guy wouldn't kill to be with a girl that flexible?" asked Happy, as they stared at Brooklyn.

"I wouldn't kick her out of *my* bed," piped up Hopper.

"Gross, Hopper!" moaned Happy and Apple in unison.

Brooklyn could stand on one leg, holding the other leg in the air next to her ear, without wobbling, for many, many minutes. She unfolded herself and went back to simply lying on her back in the middle of the hallway. It was a pose called Sivasana, a position Brooklyn always went into when she was feeling stressed out. She looked like a corpse, she was so still.

"Hey, get over here!" Happy yelled to Brooklyn.

Brooklyn picked herself up from her mat as if she was getting up from a nap, grabbed her purple yoga bag, and slowly came over.

"The past doesn't matter. The future doesn't matter. It's all about the present," said Brooklyn to herself, as she took a seat near her friends. "I will remain in the present."

Unlike Happy and Apple, Brooklyn just couldn't get good grades. Her attention span was about zero when it came to studying, because her plan was to move to India when she was old enough and study with the yogis, and she figured she didn't need good grades for that. She spent more of her time at school doing yoga than attending class.

"I'm just trying to get to the state of Ananda," Brooklyn sighed, which Apple knew, from past Brooklyn-talk, meant "bliss."

"Good luck with that," Happy said.

"Hey, Apple," said Hopper. Hopper was a walking, talking ad for Calvin Klein underwear—he was that good-looking. And he had the ego to match. He was munching on an apple. Apple knew what was coming and shook her head before he even started to speak.

"Do you happen to know what kind of apple this is?" Hopper asked, smirking at her.

"God, you're really an idiot, Hopper," Happy shot over her shoulder. "You know you're the only one who thinks you're clever, right?"

"Well, at least I didn't ask her about her apple pie," Hopper said, laughing.

"God, grow up, Hopper," Apple said. "How old are you, anyway? As if we couldn't make fun of your name, little frog."

"Come on, Apple. How is that pie of yours?" Hopper pressed.

"You only wish you could get near her apple pie," Happy threw back.

"Happy!" Apple shrieked.

"Hey, I'm just sticking up for you," Happy said to her.

"What about you, Happy—are you interested?" Hopper asked, winking. Happy just rolled her eyes.

"How about you, Brooklyn?" Hopper said.

Brooklyn, unlike Happy, started to laugh. She glanced at her friends. "I'm sorry. But Hopper is kind of funny," she said, putting a hand over her mouth. "Sorry!"

Thankfully, Hopper had moved on, to torture some other students with what he considered his "sense of humor." It was amazing what you could get away with when you were so good-looking. But not as good-looking as Zen, Apple thought, sneaking a glance at Zen, who was reading a car magazine.

"So, now that that moron is gone, tell me, did you find out what the shows are this week?" Happy whispered to Apple. "And how I get on the show?"

"Um, yeah. I said I would, and I did. You owe me that pair of jeans now! And you'd better give them to me soon. Okay, what were they again? There's one on 'Torn between Two Lovers,' um, and 'Men Who Mooch Off Their Women' . . . oh yeah, and 'Sperm Bandits.'"

"Oh my God. These shows sound so amazing! I can't wait!" said Happy, who then glanced over at Apple. "Oh, sorry, Apple. I mean, they just sound interesting, that's all."

"Really? They sound kind of like variations on the same themes Dr. Bee Bee Berg has been rehashing for the past eight years," Apple said.

Apple had spent enough time overhearing Guy and her mother discuss possible show ideas over the years that she could practically have scheduled a season of shows herself, she thought. She knew that having a broken heart bites, and that mending a broken wrist takes less time then mending a broken heart. She had learned that there seemed to be seriously millions of smart, accomplished women who were incredibly stupid when it came to choosing men. She had learned that people really do just suddenly fall out of love. Most of all, she had learned that no matter what horrific events are happening in the world—like bombs going off in major cities, children being kidnapped, tourists being murdered—no one cared more about anything than they did about their own love lives, or lack of them. Which was why *Queen of Hearts with Dr. Bee Bee Berg* was always the top-rated show in its time slot and her books were best-sellers.

"So how do I get on?" Happy asked, grabbing both of Apple's hands excitedly.

"Well, for that, my friend, you have to get in Guy's good books," Apple explained. "He's in charge of the guests. People send him e-mails and pitch him show ideas. If he likes them, then it's as simple as that."

"Hmm," Happy said. "Interesting. I had no idea it was Guy who did that. I guess I'll just have to hang out at your place more often to suck up to him, or start composing a really good show idea."

As Apple half-listened to Happy go on about how excited she was to watch her mother's show after school, she tried to eavesdrop on the conversation that

Zen was having with Hopper, who had come back to the stairs. They were sitting two steps above Happy and Apple. It was time to make a move. Apple's mouth suddenly felt very dry, as if she had been in the desert for days.

"Hey, Zen," Apple started, looking up. "How are you today?"

She couldn't believe she'd just done that. She felt so proud starting up a conversation with her crush. She even tried to look him in the eyes.

"Oh, hey, Apple," Zen answered. "So I guess you recognize me today?"

Apple felt her face starting to turn red. "Yes, of course I recognize you. I guess I was just a little surprised to see you yesterday. And I was tired, too."

Okay, this was good, thought Apple. We're talking. It's all about baby steps. Zen looked as sweet as he had the day before, Apple thought. His loosely curled blond hair was now almost shoulder-length, and he looked as hot as the characters on *Minors in Malibu*. He looked *yummy*.

"Don't worry, Apple. I didn't take it personally," Zen said, giving her that half-smile. That dimple, thought Apple, is going to be the death of me.

"What are you guys talking about?" Happy asked.

"Oh, nothing. So, Zen, how was the Land Down Under really?" Apple asked him, moving on. "It must be so weird to be back here after so much time."

"Well, I went surfing almost every day, like I said. That was pretty cool," Zen said.

"Fun!" Apple said, and then her mind went blank.

Think, Apple, think. Think of something to say to him, on the same subject. Just say anything to keep up this conversation. Do not have a repeat of yesterday.

"Well, I like to swim," Apple said. When she thought about surfing, she thought about water. And when she thought about water, she thought about swimming. And that was it! God, she was lame.

Just then, thank God, the first bell rang. There was a mad rush of students gathering their bags and note-books to head to the first class of the new semester.

Okay, that didn't go exactly as planned, Apple thought, as she stood up and looked at her timetable. That was far from an easy-breezy conversation. And does an actual conversation have to last more than twenty seconds? But the day is still young. There should be plenty more opportunity to cozy up to Zen.

"Come on, Apple. We both have math right now. Let's go," Happy said, grabbing her arm and leading her away.

"Um, I guess I'll see you later, Zen?" Apple called out.

"Sure, Apple. See you later," Zen said.

Happy and Apple walked down the hallway to their class, Happy still holding onto Apple's arm.

"Apple, did you notice anything different about Zen?" Happy asked.

"Different? What do you mean?" asked Apple, pre-tending she had no clue what Happy was getting at but feeling herself, again, turning pink at the very sound of his name.

"Oh my God. Are you blind? He looks amazing! I never noticed how good-looking he was. Who knew? You get some contact lenses and a surfer body and a tan, and, poof, six months later you're hot. Man, he's even hotter than that lifeguard," Happy said.

"I don't know," Apple answered. They walked into the classroom and took seats next to each other. "I mean, I thought he looked kind of cute before, with his glasses. They made him look smart."

"Smart, schmart. Zen is hotter now than Hopper. I think he may even have a better body," Happy said dreamily.

Apple couldn't help but think about how she had only a few more hours to talk to Zen today. She had only a few more hours to get Plan Z into action.

And she couldn't believe how slowly her classes were going by. Finally, the lunchtime bell went off. Apple felt her stomach lurch. She wasn't sure if it was hunger pangs. She knew the knot in her stomach probably had more to do with the thought of trying to talk to Zen again. I am just so bad at this, she thought.

She headed to the cafeteria. You are the daughter of Dr. Bee Bee Berg, thought Apple. For God's sake, you can do this. You *know* what to do. You read the damn book!

"Hey, Brooklyn," Apple said to her friend, who was opening a plastic container full of mung beans. Brooklyn didn't eat anything that had once had a face. She always had some sort of Tupperware container full of organic healthy fare, usually some sort of bean salad, which meant her lunches often smelled like feet. "Where's Happy?"

"She just went to the washroom. She'll be back in a sec. Doesn't being back at school suck? It's almost like we didn't have a break at all," Brooklyn moaned, putting aside her smelly lunch and lying back dramatically on the bench.

"I know. I feel all tense again," Apple admitted, not exactly telling the truth about why she was tense. "God, how can you eat that stuff?" she asked Brooklyn with a hint of disgust, and then moved the beans a little farther away from her.

"I don't know. I like it. It's good for you. Why are you so tense?" Brooklyn asked. "What's up?"

"Oh, nothing," Apple answered.

"You should really think about taking up yoga," Brooklyn advised her friend. "It's the only thing that puts my body and mind at peace. Sometimes you just need to connect your mind and your heart and all will be good."

But Apple wasn't listening. Zen had walked into the cafeteria and was about to walk by their table. Now is your chance, Apple, she thought.

"Hey, Zen," Apple called out as he came closer.

"Oh, hi, Apple. Hi, Brooklyn," Zen said.

"Do you want to sit with us?" Brooklyn asked.

"Yes, there's room here," Apple added. Or she thought she did. She wasn't sure if the words had come out at all.

"Oh, I can't. I promised Hopper I'd meet him out back and shoot some hoops with him."

"Oh, you like basketball?" Apple asked, remembering the tip to try to keep him talking about something he was interested in.

"Yeah, sure. I'm *addicted* to basketball."

"I like basketball too," Apple said.

She ignored Brooklyn, but she saw her out of the corner of her eye, looking at her as if she had gone mad. Brooklyn knew she hated all sports.

"Really. Who's your favorite team?" Zen asked.

"Um, the guys who wear the green jerseys?" Apple said. There must be a team with green jerseys, Apple prayed.

"Oh, those guys," laughed Zen. "Yeah, they're my favorite team too. Well, I'd better go. Hopper is waiting for me. See you guys later."

"Say 'hi' to Hopper for me," Brooklyn called out.

Apple watched as Zen walked off. She felt stupid and deflated. Maybe she should have been reading her mother's other book, *Mistakes Not to Make, by the Queen of Hearts.*

"Have you noticed how good Zen looks?" Brooklyn asked sincerely. "It's like he's a whole new person. Did he get plastic surgery or something?" Not you too, Apple groaned inwardly.

"Sure, Brooklyn. How many fifteen-year-old boys do you know who get plastic surgery?" Apple scoffed.

"Who got plastic surgery?" Happy asked, sitting down beside them.

"I was just saying to Apple that I think Zen got plastic surgery or something. He looks so good," Brooklyn said.

"I know!" Happy exclaimed. "I was just saying that this morning. I think he's as good-looking as Hopper now."

"Well, I don't know about *that*," Brooklyn responded, and her friends looked at her. "Hey! Hopper will always be a walking Calvin Klein under-wear ad. Everyone knows that! So don't look at me like that. But Zen is definitely in the game now, I'd say. Don't you think so, Apple?" Brooklyn asked.

"I guess so," Apple said, thinking, I *absolutely freaking* think so.

"So are we coming over to your house after school today, Apple, to watch *Queen of Hearts*? Is it the Sperm Bandit show?" Happy asked, mercifully changing the subject.

"I'm not sure. I think it may be the Torn between Two Lovers show," said Apple.

"Whatever. I can't wait to watch whatever it is," said Happy.

"Why do we have to go to *my* house?" Apple asked. "Why can't we go to yours, or Brooklyn's?"

"You want to come to my house? *My* house?" Brooklyn asked. "With the Helicopter hovering around, making sure we don't spill anything, telling us that we should be spending our time doing homework instead of watching trashy television? I don't think so!"

"The Helicopter thinks my mother's show is trashy?" Apple asked, perking up.

"Don't get too excited, Apple. The Helicopter thinks *every* show on television is trashy. She even thinks the news is trashy."

"Well, we can't go to *my* house," Happy said. "My sister will be there. And you know what Sailor is like. She's a pain in the ass and will probably be blasting her music or talking on the phone nonstop. Her mere presence will annoy us, trust me. Plus, no one will be home at your house, Apple. We're going to your house," she decided. "Besides, Guy might be there, and I need him to see I'm television-worthy."

"Well, *I* don't think Guy will be there," Apple said, as the bell rang to signal the end of lunch. "He'll be at the show. But Aunt Hazel might be there. You never know."

"Oh, I love Aunt Hazel!" Happy cried. "She's just as much a character as Guy. God, Apple, your house is always so exciting. It's *fantastic.*"

If only Happy really knew what went on, thought Apple.

"Fine, we'll go to my house," Apple said. "But I can't promise that I'm going to watch the show with you."

"Oh, you know you will," Happy called out cheerfully.

After her last class, Apple headed to the front doors to meet up with Brooklyn and Happy.

Except it was not Brooklyn and Happy who were at the front doors. It was Happy and Zen, who were talking animatedly about something. Apple stopped dead before she got there, and then watched them laughing. She wondered what they were laughing about and immediately felt left out. She was shocked to find herself feeling this way. She hadn't even managed to get more than two sentences out of Zen today, let alone make him laugh like that. Apple felt sick to her stomach. Why couldn't she be more like Happy? Happy may idolize her mother, but Apple idolized Happy. Happy made everything she did seem effortless.

Apple took a deep breath and walked up to them. "Hey, guys," she said. "I'm not interrupting anything, am I?"

"There you are!" said Happy. "I thought you were going to bail. Zen was just telling me this hilarious story about the surfing lessons he took in Australia with a former champion." Happy turned her attention fully back to Zen. "I've always wanted to learn how to surf."

"You know," Zen said, speaking directly to Happy, "it's not as hard as you think. I bet you'd be pretty good at it."

"Well, I guess I'll have to put it on my list of 101 Things I Must Do Before I Die," Happy laughed, tossing her long blond hair over her shoulder and sticking her chest out a little.

"Yeah, I'd like to try surfing too," Apple said, trying to get into the conversation. She felt like a third wheel. She felt jealous, too. But why should she be feeling jealous? They were just talking.

"You should too," said Zen, not even glancing at Apple.

"I should," said Apple. And there was an uncomfortable silence. Happy and Zen were just *staring* at each other.

"Happy, we should go, if you want to make it to my house in time," Apple finally said.

"In time for what?" Zen asked. It bothered Apple that Zen was *still* looking only at Happy when he asked her that.

"Oh—we're going to Apple's house to watch her mother's show," Happy said.

"Ah, *The Queen of Hearts with Dr. Bee Bee Berg.* A must-not-miss, right?" Zen asked.

"Right!" said Happy excitedly. "I worship her! Do you watch it?"

"Can't say that I do," Zen answered. "Sorry, Apple."

"Oh, I couldn't care less," Apple said, trying to sound cool. "Where's Brooklyn?" she asked Happy.

"She bailed. She called to tell her mother she was going to your house, and her mother forced her to come home and help her grocery shop," Happy said, with a roll of her eyes.

"Well, we'd better go, Happy, if you don't want to miss the show," Apple said, trying to move things along.

"See you tomorrow, Zen? You'll have to tell me more about surfing." Happy flashed her perfect smile and wrapped her long blond hair around her fingers.

"Sure thing, Happy. Can't wait. See you tomorrow," Zen said, waving goodbye.

Hello? I'm standing right here, thought Apple, as Zen walked away. She made a mental note to search for "surfing" and "basketball" on the Internet later that night, so she too could have something to talk about with Zen. If Happy could do it, so could she. Plan Z wasn't dead yet.

six

apple and Happy plopped themselves on the couch at Apple's house, sinking into the overstuffed pillows and putting their feet up on the coffee table. Happy grabbed the remote control and clicked the big flat-screen television on, just as the theme song of *Queen of Hearts with Dr. Bee Bee Berg* began. She hummed along.

"I can't believe you're making me watch this," Apple muttered, slouching deeper into the couch.

"Hey, no one is holding a gun to your head. Why are you in such a bad mood, anyway?" asked Happy.

"I guess just being back at school and everything. I'm just tired," Apple explained. "I didn't sleep very well last night. I'm cranky."

Apple didn't want to admit that she was a little mad at her friend. Not that she wanted to be. Not that she even knew why exactly she was angry.

"I thought you couldn't wait for break to end so your mother would get back to work and you could see us again. And now here we are, watching her working. You should be thrilled. You should be—Oh, shhh. The show is starting," Happy said, leaning closer to the television.

Apple only half paid attention to her mother, who was introducing a woman named Cybil who was in love with two men at the same time. Apparently, Cybil was engaged to be married to Dave when she met Mark, who she feels may or may not be her soulmate. As her mother's voice asking, "Do you want my advice?" buzzed in the background, Apple's mind wandered. She envisioned a good conversation with Zen and wondered how she would go about getting to the next step of Plan Z—the step of getting him to want to hang out with her.

"After the break," she heard her mother say, "we'll hear from Mark and Dave how they feel about sharing the same woman."

There was a shot of the audience clapping and then it went to a commercial.

"Okay, we can talk now," said Happy, "at least until the commercial break is over. You know, I really believe you can be in love with two people at the same time. I feel bad for Cybil."

"I feel bad for Mark and Dave," Apple answered. "What kind of woman gets herself into that kind of mess? Isn't she embarrassed at all? Aren't they all embarrassed to share this story? I feel bad for all of them. It's just so personal to be sharing with so many people."

"You want to know something personal about me?" Happy asked Apple. "I think I may have a little crush myself."

"What?" Apple said, sitting up to attention. "On who?"

Apple felt her heart sink. She suspected what was coming next. She knew Happy well enough. She knew what she'd seen after school. Happy tossing her hair behind her shoulder. Happy sticking out her chest a little.

"I knew that would get your attention. I don't know. I think I might like Zen," Happy said.

"*Like* him, like him?" Apple asked, gulping. She was trying to act calm even though she felt anything but.

"Apple, you have to swear not to say anything. Promise!" Happy said. "Except to Brooklyn. But that's all!"

"When did this happen?" Apple said, trying not to sound as shocked as she was feeling. "You never even knew he existed before today. You only talked to him for, like, five minutes after school."

"Well, sometimes that's all it takes. If you have chemistry, you have chemistry, as your mother just said. And it's not true that I never knew he existed. Of course I knew he existed. We've all been going to school together forever. We've all known each other for years," Happy said defensively.

"You know what I mean," Apple said. "You've never really talked to him before, that's all I'm saying."

"Well, I did today. And he's really interesting. I mean, he just spent months in Australia surfing! I would love to do that. And then seeing him looking so different, and then actually talking to him, made me see him in a whole new light. I never knew he was so funny and so cool. And he's sweet too." Happy was practically gushing.

This cannot be happening, Apple thought. Her best friend—make that her best friend who always looked like she just walked out of the pages of a fashion magazine—could *not* have a crush on her Zen at the same time she did.

It will be okay, Apple tried to reason to herself. This is *Happy* we're talking about—Happy who has flings with lifeguards whose last names she doesn't even know. This was just Happy being carefree, friendly, and flirtatious.

She couldn't possibly really be "in like" with Zen so suddenly. Even if she was, her feelings could be gone by tomorrow.

Happy was still chattering on.

"Do you think it's strange that I like him? You can tell me the truth, Apple. What do you think?" she asked.

"No, it's just that, well, you just got out of a relationship with that lifeguard, right? Maybe you're just feeling like you need someone to fill that void." Apple could hear her mother's voice in her own.

"I told you! That was just a fling! It didn't mean anything. Zen is different. He's really—Okay, shh, the show is starting again. I need to know who Cybil will choose—Dave or Mark."

Happy had gone back to immersing herself in the love lives of others.

Apple, on the other hand, had completely stopped paying attention to the show. Her mind was on what Happy had just told her. Happy may like Zen. Happy may be into Zen.

She was so wrapped up in this thought that she didn't even notice that *Queen of Hearts* had ended and the credits were rolling.

"Can you believe she chose Dave? But I guess it's like your mother said—you choose the one you know treats *their* mother well. And you could just tell Dave was the type of guy who treats his mother well." Happy chatted away. "Crap. I think that's Sailor honking out front. I told her to come get me at six after she finished her dance class. Thanks for letting me watch, Apple. I'll see you tomorrow. And remember—do not say a word to anyone about what I told you about Zen! It may be nothing. But it sure does make going to school a little more interesting." Happy blew Apple a kiss goodbye and headed out the door.

Apple could only hope that this was true, that it was nothing. Zen was *her* reason to look forward to school. She didn't want to share that with anyone, not even Happy.

Apple headed to her room. She needed to compose herself. She needed to think. And she knew that the only way to make herself feel better was to write to ED. Writing in her private journal was the one time she felt she could collect her thoughts. It was her therapy. Just like some people liked to talk out their problems, Apple liked to write. Sitting down at her desk, Apple saw the "on" button was already lit up.

That's weird, Apple thought. Why is my computer already on? She could have sworn that she had turned it off after writing to ED that morning before going to school. She touched her mouse pad and up came her most recent ED entry, the one about her being nervous to go to school and about Plan Z and about reading her mother's book. There's no way I didn't shut this down, she thought. There's no way! Apple always made a point of turning off her computer. She started to bite her fingernails, frowning, while looking at the screen.

There was only one reason Apple could think of that her computer would be on. My mother, my damn nosy, snooping mother, she thought. How dare she!

Did her mother have no boundaries? Dr. Bee Bee Berg is the worst mother in the world, Apple thought, slamming her laptop shut. She was no longer even in the mood to write to ED. First her best friend had disappointed her, and now her mother. This day sucked. She tried to think like Brooklyn. "The future doesn't matter, the past doesn't matter. It's all about the present. Think positive thoughts and the world will respond positively back."

It was sort of right, thought Apple. I can't control the past and the fact I never could get up the nerve to talk to Zen. I can't control the future and seeing if Happy goes through with liking Zen. Right now, I'm going to concentrate on my homework. Apple picked up her knapsack and rummaged through her bag. She saw her mother's book and, rolling her eyes, threw it across her room so it hit the wall. She walked over to pick it up. Then she threw it in the trash.

seven

"*G*uess what I've spent the last hour doing?" Happy asked Apple, in a singsong voice, near the end of the week. It was early evening and Happy had phoned while Apple was lying on her bed, attempting to read a book for her English literature class. Apple hadn't been very successful at studying either. She couldn't focus on anything. She had really mostly been lying on her bed and staring at the ceiling and at the things in her room. There were ceramic apples all over her bedroom, in all sorts of sizes, and apple-shaped picture frames too. There were even stickers of apples around the border of her mirror. For as long as Apple could remember, whenever someone didn't know what to get her as a present, they bought her things with apples on them. She thought it was probably time to redecorate her room. Who needed to be reminded all the time what her name was?

Apple couldn't believe school had started only earlier this week. When nothing happens, it seems like an eternity. And nothing had happened. She had tried to speak to Zen numerous times, and he was always polite, but the conversations never lasted more than a few minutes. She had even picked up a new car magazine and handed it to him one morning, telling him she had found it and thought he might like it. All he said was "Thanks," and then he tossed it into his knapsack. She had even mentioned a movie she'd heard good things about. But Zen hadn't suggested they go see it together. He'd just said, "Maybe I'll check it out."

"I'm not good at guessing," Apple told Happy on the phone.

"Just take a guess!" Happy demanded.

"Washing your hair?" Apple guessed.

"No. Try again."

"Um, reading a magazine," Apple guessed again.

"God, you really are bad at guessing," Happy laughed. "You weren't joking."

"I know. So just tell me!" Apple demanded.

"Fine, I will. I've been messaging back and forth with Zen," she said.

"What?" Apple said, sitting up now.

"I know! When I got home from school today, I logged onto my computer to see if I could order this pair of boots and suddenly an e-mail popped up from Zen. He even sent me pictures of him surfing in Australia. You should see him with his shirt off," Happy giggled.

Apple was stunned. All *she* had been doing was trying to study.

Apple had thought that maybe studying would force her to get her mind off the fact that Plan Z had gotten her nowhere in the past four days. Apple wondered if her mother's self-help advice had ever worked for anyone, because it certainly hadn't worked for her. Why was something that seemed so easy on paper so hard in practice?

"Wow. I can't believe he did that!" Apple said, hoping her tone came off more like excitement for her friend than like shock that her Super-Sized Zen Crush was IM'ing Happy instead of her.

"I know! So I wrote him back and we just started chatting away," continued Happy.

"About what?" Apple asked. What did Happy and Zen have to chat about, anyway?

"Oh, school, our families, stuff like that. I even told him about Dr. Caffeine."

"You did not!" Apple said, shocked.

Dr. Caffeine had been Happy's therapist for years. Happy called her Dr. Caffeine because she offered her a can of pop or a coffee every time Happy came in for her weekly appointment. Seeing a therapist was the only thing Happy's parents demanded that she and Sailor do on a regular basis. Apple supposed they felt guilty they were never around, and that making Happy and Sailor see a therapist made them feel like better parents somehow, like they really did care.

Happy had never told anyone except Brooklyn and Apple about her weekly appointments with Dr. Caffeine. She was embarrassed about them. So it surprised Apple that Happy had told Zen, a classmate she had only started to have conversations with. How was he suddenly in the inner circle of Happy's secrets?

"He's just so easy to talk to," Happy gushed. "He makes it so easy to open up to him. He's a really good listener. He's kind of like you, actually. And he's so sweet too. You're not going to believe what he's planning to do." Happy paused, waiting to be asked.

"Tell me," Apple said sullenly.

"Well, you know that clothing drive the school is organizing, where they're setting up a table at the country club to collect clothes for the homeless shelters?"

"Yeah," Apple said. She vaguely remembered hearing an announcement about it over the speakers at school and seeing some posters on the walls.

"Well, he's actually thinking about doing it. He's giving up his free time to sit at a table in the country club! It just shows that he has a kind heart, you know? Here I am ordering designer boots online because I'm too lazy even to go to a store, and he's planning to collect people's old clothes to give to shelters. It just shows how thoughtful he is, doesn't it?"

"Yeah, it does." Apple really had to agree. Not like she hadn't known that. She had followed Zen's moves for years. Apple knew that Zen was always volunteering whenever the school needed people to raise money for charity or to answer phones for fundraising drives.

"Well, I just had to let you know," Happy told Apple. "I had to tell *someone*, and of course it had to be you! And now I'd better get back to reading too, because I just spent an hour and a half IM'ing with Zen."

"I thought you said you only chatted for an hour," Apple said, feeling herself falling into a worse mood by the second.

"Well, it was more like two hours. But it seemed like ten minutes. Love you!" Happy said, and hung up.

Apple threw her phone down on her bed and walked over to her computer to write to ED.

Dear ED,

I can't believe what is happening. It's like my mother always says. Sometimes life is just not fair. I hate to admit it, but I'm really distressed. Happy just called and told me she had been chatting with Zen—yes, MY Zen—for almost two hours! It's not like I wasn't around to IM with. I hate myself for saying this, I do, but it just seems everything comes so easily for Happy. I don't know, maybe it's like my mother always says to Crazy Aunt Hazel—that when you least expect it, that's when you meet someone. Maybe the problem was that for years, I was WAITING for something to happen with Zen. Happy wasn't waiting. And something is definitely starting to happen with her and Zen. Then again, it was just instant messaging. Maybe I'm just overreacting. I want to be happy for my best friend but . . .

Apple suddenly stopped typing. Her mother had snooped in her electronic diary just a few days before. How could she have forgotten? This was the kind of problem her mother would totally get off on, too—a girl being in love with a guy she has never told, who apparently was showing interest in her best friend instead. There was no way she was going to let her mother find out what she was going through. No, Apple was not like the rest of the Bergites—what Apple called

Dr. Bee Bee Berg's cult-like followers. She didn't like to share her problems with anyone, especially not her mother. She wasn't even sure if Zen's chatting with Happy *was* a problem. Maybe they were just becoming friends. But she was still pissed at her mother for daring to sneak into her room to read her diary. The only way to get back at her mother for snooping was to try and trap her in the act. Apple deleted what she'd written about Zen and Happy, and started to type again.

Dear ED,
You can forget about everything I wrote about Zen the other day. I don't like him anymore. It was all just a silly phase. I have discovered true love now—the love that only a REAL man can inspire. You know, a VERY mature man. I'm in love with Mr. Kelly. That's right. I'm in serious love with my math teacher. I know this sounds weird, considering how much I hate math, but I'm really starting to enjoy class. Especially since Mr. Kelly is so hot. So you can forget about Plan Z. My new plan is to get Mr. Kelly to fall as deeply in love with me as I am with him. It is possible, you know, ED. He is single. And gorgeous. And he's not that old. He may be, like, only 35. And he seems to really like me. Every time I put up my hand in class, he chooses me. I swear, I love watching him write out math questions on the blackboard. He has the most gorgeous hands. Hands that I would love to feel all over my body. I will keep you posted, ED. I promise. Oh, I can't wait for math class! In fact, I may just become a mathematician one day. That's how into math I am now. Well, that's how much I'm into Mr. Kelly!

I'm done with high school boys. I want a real man, not a silly high school boy.

Apple smirked, rereading what she'd just written. She thought it sounded believable. There was no way her mother wouldn't mention something about *this* fake diary entry. It was like her mother's advice to women who take back men who cheat on them: once a cheater, always a cheater. Or was it that leopards can never change their spots? Whatever it was, Apple thought, once a snooper, always a snooper. Her mother couldn't change her spots. Once she read it, her mother would *have* to admit that she had read Apple's private diary. Apple purposely left her entry on the screen and didn't shut down her computer. Her mother would feel as embarrassed as Apple did now knowing that someone had read her private thoughts. Then her mother would, for sure, butt out of Apple's life, maybe for good. I have no choice, thought Apple. I can't trust writing to ED again. I have to be super protective now. I've been burned.

eight

*G*alvanized by the night before's conversation with Happy, Apple knew that she really had to focus on Plan Z. When the lunch bell rang, she caught up with Zen and asked him straight out, "Come eat lunch with me." She was sick of being so pathetic. Happily, Zen agreed, and they walked into the cafeteria together. Unfortunately, Apple's excitement lasted only a moment. Zen spotted Happy and Brooklyn and started heading toward them. There was no way Apple could suggest now that they eat somewhere else—it was too late for that. There was nothing she could do but follow.

"Can we join you?" Zen asked.

"Of course!" Happy said, sliding over to make room for both of them.

Happy was daintily devouring a chopped salad. Brooklyn, as usual, was scoffing down some sort of bean dish. Despondently, Apple started to unwrap her tuna salad sandwich.

"Great," said Zen, smiling at Happy. "You know, Happy, you smell like peach."

"It's my conditioner," Happy laughed, tossing back her hair. "Do you like it?"

"Oh, yeah. It's making me really hungry. Let me smell it again," he said, gently grabbing a chunk of Happy's beautiful thick blond hair and inhaling deeply. "Yup. I'm definitely hungry for a peach now."

Brooklyn and Apple raised their eyebrows at one another. There was no doubt about it—Zen was flirting with Happy. Apple suddenly felt anything but hungry. Her lunch was ruined, and she tossed her sandwich into a nearby garbage can.

"Let me smell *your* hair," Happy said to Zen, leaning toward him. "Not too bad either," she told him. "I like a man who uses a nice-smelling shampoo."

Apple couldn't take it a second longer. She jumped up, wiping crumbs off her pants. "Excuse me, you guys," she said, interrupting the flirtation. "I forgot one of my books in the classroom. I'd better go get it."

"Wait. I'm coming with you," Brooklyn said, grabbing her yoga mat. "Peace and love!"

Apple and Brooklyn walked out of the cafeteria. Neither Happy nor Zen seemed to notice they had left. They didn't even say goodbye.

"It seems someone and someone wanted to be alone," Brooklyn said. "God, if they get together, they'll be like the next Brangelina! They're both too good-looking," she added. "The only thing that would be more good-looking would be Happy and Hopper."

"You don't think they actually like each other, do you?" Apple asked Brooklyn.

"It seemed like they *very much* were into each other. I was about to tell them to get a hotel room. So where did you leave your book?" Brooklyn asked Apple.

When Apple didn't respond, Brooklyn laughed. "I knew it! I knew it! You saw that they wanted to be left alone too. You just made up that excuse to get away."

"I did not! Happy is a flirt," Apple protested. "She's always been a flirt. It doesn't mean anything. I honestly thought I forgot my book, but I didn't." Brooklyn wasn't exactly right. Apple just felt awful that there she was, probably smelling like tuna, and Happy smelled like peach. She made a mental note to ask Happy what kind of shampoo she used. She wanted to smell like peach too, not like fish.

"Sure, whatever," Brooklyn said, heading to the staircase. "You're not going to believe what my mother did. She took away my cell phone! Can you believe the Helicopter took away my phone? Apparently, calling the theater to check on movie times is not considered an emergency. Apple? Apple? Did you hear what I just said?" Brooklyn shook Apple's arm.

Apple's attention was on a table set up in the hallway.

An older student named Poppy, who Apple knew was in Sailor's year, was calling out, "Last day to sign up for the clothing drive! Help out those less fortunate and contribute your time. It's easy!"

Suddenly, a thought came to Apple. She needed to get Zen alone with her, and if Happy was always around, that would never happen. But Happy had told her that Zen had signed up for the clothing drive. This was her chance!

"You know what, Brooklyn? I'm going to help out with the clothing drive," Apple said.

"Really?" Brooklyn raised her eyebrows at Apple, then added, "I mean, that's great!"

"Yes, I am. It's a good thing to do," Apple said, "and I have the time. It's good karma, as you always say."

Apple walked over to the sign-up table, with Brooklyn following.

"I think I may be interested. What do I have to do?" Apple asked Poppy.

"Hey, you're Apple, right?" Poppy asked.

"Yes."

"I love your hair. I've always wanted to tell you that. And Dr. Bee Bee Berg is your mother, right? I love her show! Do you think she could mention the clothing drive on her show?" Poppy asked.

"Um, it's a show about *relationships*," Brooklyn said to Poppy.

"I know! I've only watched it like every day for five years now! I just thought Apple could maybe mention it to her mother or something. If Dr. Bee Bee Berg threw her support behind this, we'd kick butt," Poppy said.

"My mother is pretty busy," Apple told Poppy, "but I'll ask."

She couldn't bring herself to just say no to Poppy. While it was one thing to complain to her friends, Apple would never complain about her mother to people she didn't know. Not that Apple would ever ask her mother to mention the clothing drive. Her mother wouldn't have the time anyway.

"But if you want my help, too," she added, "I'll be willing. So, what does this require exactly?"

"Well, you just write your name and e-mail address on this sheet, and we'll be in touch with you. It will only require a few hours after school for a couple of weeks, whenever you can find the time, and you'll really be doing a good deed for those who are less fortunate than us."

"Does she have to call people and ask for their old clothes or something?" Brooklyn asked.

"No, we already have students calling parents right now. All you have to do, Apple, is sit at a table at the country club, where we're going to set up shop, collect the clothes, and bring them back to school. It's very easy. All you have to do is donate your time, really," Poppy said. "Your family are already members of the club anyway, so you know where it is, right?"

"Yes," Apple nodded. "Okay, I'm in. Can you please hand me the sign-up sheet?"

"Great! Here you go," Poppy said, handing Apple a clipboard.

Apple quickly scanned the dozen or so names of students who had signed up for the clothing drive. There it was, near the top of the page. Zen's name. She ran her finger lovingly over his handwriting. It made her feel close to him.

Apple wrote her name and e-mail address at the bottom of the list.

"I can't believe you're doing this, Apple," said Brooklyn. "You know, I admire you. It's such a good thing to do. You're such a good person. I think it shows real growth and maturity. And you're right—it will bring you good karma. You do good things, and karma will do good things to you."

Okay, thought Apple, so I'm not signing up for truly altruistic reasons. But I'm still going to help people. Maybe Brooklyn was right, too, about karma. Apple thought that maybe some higher power would appreciate her volunteer efforts and get Zen to notice her. And then maybe after she and Zen collected clothes, they could grab a burger or something at the club's burger shack. Apple smiled. Plan Z was back in action, baby.

Brooklyn grabbed the clipboard from Apple's hand to check to see who else had signed up. "Hey, Zen has signed up too."

"He has?" Apple said, trying to act surprised.

"Yup, right here," said Brooklyn, pointing out Zen's name. "You know, I'd love to help out. But what with all my schoolwork, and working on my yoga poses, I'm too busy. Plus the Helicopter would never let me do it, I'm sure. But Apple, you should volunteer at the same time as Zen. At least that way you might have some fun."

"Is that possible?" Apple asked Poppy. "I mean, you did say you have two people sit at the same table."

"Let me put a note down. I think I'll be able to organize it. Leave it up to me. For the daughter of Dr. Bee Bee Berg, I'll make it happen," Poppy said with a smile.

Apple had to admit that sometimes being the daughter of the Queen of Hearts had its perks.

♡

Apple headed home after school, enjoying the half-hour walk, feeling like a million dollars. She was excited again about her Plan Z, which was *finally* moving forward.

She opened the front door to find Aunt Hazel sprawled out on the couch reading *US Weekly*.

"What are you doing here all by yourself?" Apple asked her aunt. "Do you spend your entire days here? Don't you have somewhere else to hang out? What, did you just come back here after you dropped me off this morning?" She looked around. All around Aunt Hazel were bowls and glasses and tissues. It looked like she hadn't left the couch in hours. She was always such a slob. "It looks like a storm passed through here," Apple said.

"Apple, please. I took the day off. I took a mental health day," her aunt said.

"A mental day? Is that like a sick day?" Apple asked.

"I needed a mental *health* day."

"Guy trouble?" Apple asked her aunt. As if she even had to ask!

"Kyle broke up with me," her aunt said blandly.

"Kyle? Who's *Kyle*?" Apple asked. She couldn't remember a Kyle.

"Oh, just some guy I met last night," was Hazel's answer.

"I thought you were getting over Rupert!" Apple gasped.

"His name was Roger!" her aunt yelled.

"Right. Whatever. Who is Kyle then?" Apple asked. Suddenly, seeing her dreary crazy aunt was deflating her high.

Aunt Hazel sighed. "I need to tell you what happened," she said to Apple.

"No, really, it's okay. You don't have to tell me. Really. You can keep it to yourself. That's fine by me," Apple pleaded. "Some things a person should just keep to themselves."

"No, I *want* to tell you. I need to talk about it," her aunt insisted, much to Apple's dismay.

"Are you sure you want to be telling this stuff to me?" Apple asked. "Not that I'm not interested. It's just that I'm only fifteen. I'm not sure I'm old enough to hear all the gory details."

Her aunt ignored her and continued talking.

"We had a great night. We laughed. We talked. He invited me to spend the night at his place. Then this morning, after a wildly passionate night where—"

"Can we just skip over the more intimate details please," Apple moaned, interrupting.

"Right. Well, this morning Kyle was taking a shower and I couldn't help myself. I started sneaking around his place. I mean, how was I to know that he takes two-minute showers? He caught me while I was looking in an old shoebox in his closet. He kicked me out," Aunt Hazel told her, tears now running down her face.

"Well, what did you find?" Apple asked.

"What do you mean?" her aunt asked.

"In the shoebox? What did you find while you were sneaking around in his closet in the shoebox? Was it dirty pictures or something?" Apple asked, genuinely curious now.

"No. It was just shoes," Crazy Aunt Hazel said, before really breaking down.

Oh . . . my . . . God, Apple thought. She couldn't help but burst out laughing.

"I'm sorry, but you have to admit, it's kind of funny," she finally said. "Have you told my mother?"

"Yes. Of course," Aunt Hazel said.

"And what did the great Dr. Bee Bee Berg say to you?"

"Oh, you know your mother. Same old. Same old. She advised me that men don't find women who sneak around in their closets very cute at all. She advised me that it was psychotic. She advised me that I have 'trust issues,'" her aunt said, mocking her sister. "You know what your mother's like."

"You think?" Apple asked, and started to laugh again. "I can't believe I'm going to say this, but I think Mom has a point."

"Okay, enough. I know I'm pathetic. I just came here to be alone in my patheticness. But I'm going now. Your dad called. He's staying late at the office but wants you to call him. There's dinner in the kitchen."

"What? There is?" Apple asked. She was used to making herself a bowl of cereal for dinner.

"Don't get too excited. It's just a pizza that I ordered and ate half of. Double cheese. Okay, I'm out of here. Enjoy your night."

Apple walked into the kitchen, enjoying the peace and quiet that was so rare around the Berg household. Apple didn't often have the entire house to herself, but she knew it probably wouldn't last long.

She called her father and had a brief, friendly chat. He sounded a bit sad on the phone, and mentioned he was going to play nine holes, which broke Apple's heart. It was as if he wanted to spend as much time away from the house as he possibly could. He usually played golf only on the weekends.

She sat on the couch and turned on the television, ready to plop in her *Minors in Malibu* DVD. The characters on *Minors in Malibu* got together all the time. It gave her hope, even though she knew it was just a television show.

Instead she heard a key in the front door, and jumped to attention, wondering who it could be. Maybe it was Aunt Hazel coming back to moan some more about Ken, or Kyle, or whatever his name was. Or maybe she forgot something? Maybe it was Guy, coming over to attend to some of her mother's e-mail. Maybe her father had decided not to golf today after all.

"Apple," her mother said, walking through the doors. "I'm glad you're here."

"Don't you have some event to be at?" Apple asked. "What are you doing home so early? It's only seven."

"Not tonight. Well, I did, but I canceled at the last minute. And you know, I think Alice Cooper was going to be there. Your father would have died."

Great, Apple thought, she probably felt she had to spend some quality time with her daughter. It was so not necessary, Apple thought.

"I want to talk to you about something very sensitive," her mother began, sitting down on the couch next to Apple, grabbing the remote from her hand, and clicking off the television.

"Hey!" Apple said. "I was watching that!"

"I'm sorry, but this is important," her mother said sternly.

"Mom! This isn't going to be a sex talk, is it? I mean, we already had that conversation when I was eleven, and then when I was twelve, then again when I was thirteen."

"No, it's not a sex talk. Well, not exactly," her mother said.

"What is it now, Mom? I really should get up and do some homework, so you're going to have to make this quick," Apple pressed.

"Apple, high school is a confusing time," her mother began. "Being fifteen is a confusing time. I get that."

"And your point is?" Apple asked, trying to get the conversation moving faster. The sooner it really started, the sooner it would end.

"My point is that while you may think you're an adult, you are not. You are still a little girl—*my* little girl," she added.

"And your point is?" Apple asked again. What was her mother rambling on about now?

"Apple, don't be sarcastic. It's important and healthy to get to know people your own age. It's important to hang around guys your own age," her mother said, wringing her hands.

"Mom, you're not trying to tell me to get a boyfriend again, are you?" Apple asked. "I told you there's no one I'm interested in."

"No, but I'm telling you that you may learn some-thing from hanging around boys your own age. That you will want to have gone through all the things other fifteen-year-old girls go through with fifteen-year-old boys. I just don't want you to ever have to regret missing out on that. You should enjoy your youth now, with other . . . youthful people."

Apple, at that instant, suddenly understood what her mother was trying to get at. It was patently clear that her mother had read her electronic diary entry—her *fake* diary entry—about her crush—her *fake* crush—on Mr. Kelly, her math teacher, just as Apple had suspected she would.

"Okay, and . . . ," Apple said, playing along, trying not to smile. She rolled her eyes for effect. Let's just see, she thought, if she's going to admit what she's done, that she rudely went and read my *private* diary entry. She should totally apologize, Apple thought.

"Well, Apple, I'm just worried that you're missing out on a critical and pivotal stage in your life. Like I said, I don't want you to have any regrets, or to do anything stupid," Dr. Berg told her daughter.

"Stupid? Stupid like what?" Apple pressed her mother, who was starting to look uncomfortable. It was rare indeed for Dr. Bee Bee Berg to look uncomfortable while interrogating someone. She was a pro, after all.

Apple knew her mother was uncomfortable because she knew she had done something wrong, namely sneak into Apple's private documents.

"Stupid like . . . stupid like not giving boys your age a chance," her mother said.

"Mom, I don't know what you're getting at. But I really do have to get to my homework. This conversation is over." Apple got up and headed up the stairs. Wow, she thought. She had always wanted to say, "This conversation is over."

"Apple, wait!" her mother demanded, standing up. She had a concerned look on her face.

"No, we're done talking. I can't believe you!" Apple snapped at her mother.

"I was just trying to help," her mother said.

"I don't need your help!" Apple stormed into her room and slammed the door. As she threw herself onto the bed, she heard, faintly, her mother still nattering at her. Apple was right, and she couldn't help but feel slightly triumphant. It was just as she had expected, that her mother would want to talk about her fake diary entry. But she was also angry. How dare her mother sneak a peak at her diary and then interrogate her as if *she* was the one who had done something wrong!

"Trust me on this," she heard her mother yell through the door. "I'm your mother!"

Apple got under her covers. Her suspicions about her mother had proved right. To make matters even worse, her mother was being pushy, demanding that she date boys her own age. Not only was her mother a sneak, but she was overbearing too. Apple was more desperate than ever to keep every thought to herself from now on. No matter what.

nine

$\mathcal{A}$fter her Aunt Hazel dropped her off at school the next morning, Apple headed to the spiral staircase. Brooklyn, Happy, and Zen were already sitting there.

"Hey, Apple!" Happy said immediately. "You didn't tell me you volunteered to do the clothing drive at the club! You should have told me—we could have done it together!"

"Oh, well, it was a spur-of-the-moment thing," Apple told her friend, hoping that her face was not turning red. She was not a good liar. "Brooklyn and I were just walking by the table yesterday and I thought, 'Why not?' And plus I know how busy you are with acting classes. I didn't think you'd have the time."

"I got an e-mail last night telling me we'll be watching the table together," Zen said to Apple.

"Me too! How lucky is it that we got paired up together?" Apple asked Zen. "I mean, it's lucky that we at least know each other. It would suck to be stuck next to someone you didn't know, if you know what I mean," she continued clumsily.

"That's true," Zen agreed.

"Well, it sounds to *me* like it could be fun," Happy said, pouting. "I wish I was volunteering too."

"It's probably not too late to sign up," Zen told her. "You could just come along with Apple and me today. I'm sure no one would mind. Or you could just hang out and we could meet you after at the burger shack or something."

Zen seemed to perk up at the idea, and Happy was beaming at Zen's eagerness to include her.

Great, thought Apple. That's just great. She felt a pang of guilt. Happy was her best friend. She should *want* to hang out with Happy. Happy and Apple had spent many afternoons lying by the pool at the club, for years, since they were kids.

"Oh, but Apple's right," said Happy. "I just can't. I really don't have the time." Immediately Apple felt relieved. Then she felt guilty for feeling relieved. Why did she always end up feeling guilty over something?

"Even today I have somewhere to be," Happy added, sounding disappointed. "I can't get out of it." Apple knew that Happy's appointment was a session with Dr. Caffeine.

"Well," said Zen, "I guess I'll meet you by the front doors after school, Apple, and we'll take it from there. I think North said he was heading over to the club with his brother, so we can catch a ride with them, if that's cool with you."

"That's cool," Apple said, trying to be nonchalant.

"I've got to head to class now," he said, though he didn't really look like he wanted to leave.

"Oh, I'll come with you," said Brooklyn. "We have science now, right?"

Apple was left alone with Happy, but she couldn't read the expression on her friend's face. It was one Apple hadn't ever seen before. Was Happy that upset that she had to go see her shrink? Or was she really that disappointed that she hadn't signed up to volunteer . . .

"Apple," began Happy, "you have to do me a biggie."

"What?" Apple asked. The last time Happy asked her to do a "biggie" it was about asking how she could get on *Queen of Hearts*. "Please don't ask me again about getting on the show. And you never gave me those jeans!"

"No, no. I'm over that. But you have to chat up Zen for me. You have to tell him how wonderful I am. You have to get some information out of him," Happy said, almost desperately. "And I promise to bring you the jeans."

"Information? What do you mean?" asked Apple. "I'm not good at that, Happy—you know that. I'm so bad at getting things out of people."

"Just mention my name in conversation and see what he says. Just pretend you're your mother for a minute and start asking him some questions. Please, Apple. Pretty please? Somehow just work me into the conversation. It'll be really easy," she said, grabbing Apple's hands tightly.

"But why?" Apple asked her friend. "Why do you want me to do this?"

"So I can know how he feels about me?" Happy responded. "I can't read him."

Apple had never seen Happy in insecure mode before. What was going on with her friend?

"Why do you care?" Apple said to her. "You've never cared before about how people felt about you. You didn't care about the lifeguard. And it's why we love you. We love the fact that you couldn't give a rat's ass about what people think about you. It's what makes you *you*," she said, releasing her hands from Happy's tight grip.

"I know. I know. I hate myself for even asking," Happy said, turning her face away from Apple. "But please? Could you?"

"I don't know, Happy."

"Oh, come on, Apple. Can you just do this for me?" Happy pleaded.

How can I *not* do this for Happy? thought Apple, especially since her friend looked . . . what? She looked like she very much needed Apple to do this for her. It pained Apple to see her friend looking . . . insecure? borderline desperate?

"Okay, fine. I'll ask. But I'm not making any promises."

"Thanks, Apple. You're the best!" Happy said, throwing her arms around Apple's neck. "That's all I'm asking for."

After school, Apple headed to the front doors. She saw Zen standing there—and Happy walking off, her blond ponytail bouncing behind her and a happy jaunt in her step. Obviously, her friend had perked up since that morning.

"You just missed Happy," Zen told her when she walked up to him. Was it just her imagination, or was Zen beaming? He looked like he was trying to swallow his big smile. It wasn't working.

"So, are we meeting North?" Apple asked.

"Yup. He's in the parking lot waiting for us. We'd better go. Our chariot awaits," Zen said, sweeping his arms in front of him, then opening the door for her to exit first.

"Great!" Apple said. "Let's go have some fun!"

"What?" Zen said.

"Well, I mean volunteering should also be fun," Apple said.

Why did the words coming from her mouth always sound so moronic when she tried to talk to Zen? She was positive that he was looking at her like she was an oddball.

Apple piled in the back seat of the big SUV and stayed quiet while the boys talked about golf scores. Apple couldn't contribute to this conversation at all. She didn't even bother trying.

North's brother dropped them off and parked in the visitor's parking lot at the club.

"I'm going to go pump some iron," North said, sounding like Hulk Hogan. "Catch you guys later."

Apple and Zen walked into the lobby and saw a table was set up for them in a corner.

"Hey, guys!" said Poppy, who was sitting at the table. "It's your shift now. All you have to do is take the clothes that people drop off, go through them, fold them, and put them in the marked boxes. And no stealing! It's hard, because there's some good stuff people are giving away. Then, when you're done, take the boxes out to the valet station. Someone is going to come pick them up later. Ta ta," Poppy said, and left with a wave.

"I guess all we have to do is sit here, then, and wait?" Apple asked Zen, when they were alone.

"Yeah, it probably won't get really busy until dinner time, I imagine," Zen said.

Every night the club had a buffet-style dinner, meant for families. The kids would run around on the back lawn, which led to the golf course, while their parents sipped cocktails and mingled with each other.

"So, what's up?" Apple asked Zen, pulling up a chair for him. Zen was even shyer than Apple was. Apple knew it had to be her to start the conversation or they'd really sit there in silence.

"Oh, you know, the usual. Just school and stuff," Zen answered.

"Yeah. Don't you hate being back at school?" Apple asked.

"Actually, surprisingly, it's not as boring as I remember," Zen said. "I'm not having as bad a time as I expected I would coming back."

"Really?"

"Yup."

"I mean, when I ran into you on the street the day before break ended, you said you were dreading going back," Apple said, confused.

"Yeah, I was. But I'm not now. It's kind of nice to be back, actually."

Apple didn't know what to say. She certainly didn't want to ask Zen why he was so happy about being back at school, for fear of the answer.

They sat beside each other in silence. She swore she could hear the tennis balls bouncing on the tennis courts outside, and the click of the pool cues. She swore she could even hear a golf ball rolling across the course. But this was her do-or-die moment. This was when Plan Z was supposed to be in full-on action. She was finally alone with Zen, which is what she had hoped for all along. She had to talk about *something* or else the next hour would be painful.

What else did they have in common? Apple was desperate to make some sort of connection with Zen.

It came down to Happy. Apple gulped. They clearly had Happy in common, and she had promised her friend she would talk about her. Why not kill two birds with one stone? It was better to talk about Happy than to not talk about anything and sit in this uncomfortable silence. It wasn't the kind of silence she enjoyed.

"Isn't Happy so pretty?" Apple found herself asking.

She saw Zen perk up. She was torn. At least he seemed to be interested in talking to her now, but why did he have to perk up when the conversation was about her best friend? Once she got him interested, though, she could move on to other things, things that didn't have to focus around Happy.

"She's beautiful! I never knew how beautiful she really was," Zen said. "She makes me laugh, too."

"Yeah, she can be really funny," agreed Apple.

"And sweet," Zen added. "I always thought she was kind of spoiled. But she's not, really. I mean she is, but she doesn't act like it, you know?"

"Of course I know. I'm her best friend!"

"And she seems like she'd be fun," he went on. Was he asking a question?

"Oh, she is," Apple said. "You're not the only one who thinks so. She's a live-for-the-moment kind of girl, you know what I mean?" She knew she was entering uncool territory—because she already knew what she was planning on saying.

"Not exactly. Maybe. What do you mean?" Zen asked.

"Well, take the lifeguard for example," Apple said, leaning in toward Zen. She was close enough to smell him. Happy was right—he did smell good.

"The lifeguard?" Zen asked, confused.

"Yeah, the lifeguard she had a fling with over winter break in Mexico. Didn't she tell you?" Apple asked. "I mean, that's what I was talking about."

Apple felt horrible. She knew she was somehow betraying Happy, but it wasn't like Happy had ever told her that the lifeguard fling was a secret or anything. And, Apple figured, Happy was the one who had asked her to talk about her, to bring her up in conversation. She was just doing as told. Happy had, after all, practically forced Apple to talk about her to Zen. How else was she to do it?

"Um, I don't think so," Zen said. "She never mentioned anything about a lifeguard."

"Well, she had this wild fling with this super-sexy lifeguard. She didn't even ask his last name! But that's

Happy for you. Like you said, she's really into having a good time," Apple said nonchalantly.

"I see," Zen said, more slowly now.

"Yeah, she likes her flings. Nothing too, too serious. She's sweet, though, isn't she?"

"Yeah."

"And she's really funny, like you said," Apple continued.

"Yeah."

"And she's super good-looking, like you said."

"Yeah."

She could tell Zen's mind was working overtime on what she had just told him.

"Just forget what I said about the lifeguard," she said now. "It was just a fling! She really did it just to piss off her sister. I don't think it meant anything to her. No, I'm *sure* it didn't," she added, trying to cheer him up.

Apple knew she needed to change the subject. "I think this is really good you're helping out like this," she told Zen. "I just think you have the best heart."

"Well, you're here too," said Zen, but sullenly.

The guilt! It was killing her. She was supposed to talk up her friend, not talk her down.

"You know, I'm really not feeling well all of a sudden," Zen said. "Maybe I'm coming down with something. Let's continue this another time. I think I really need to get out of here."

"Really? But what about the clothing that people are going to drop off?" Apple asked. She hoped he didn't hear the whine in her voice, like she did.

"Oh, don't worry about it. I'm sure you can handle it on your own," he said, pushing back his chair loudly and getting up.

How could Apple save this disastrous turnaround? What was it she had read in her mother's book? Something about giving out compliments?

"Well, like I said, I really think you are great for doing this, even if you're not feeling well and need to go. I totally understand."

"Um . . ."

"I do," Apple pressed. "You're great!"

"Thanks. Sorry, I guess I'm just not good at getting compliments. It makes me feel uncomfortable. I'm going to just go home and take a nap or something. You sure you don't mind?"

"No, it's fine. It's fine," said Apple. "I hope you feel better."

"How are you going to get home? Can you get somebody to pick you up?" Zen asked. Apple was devastated that he was leaving and even lying about coming down with something. She knew she was responsible for putting him in a bad mood, and yet he still cared enough to ask *her* if she'd be okay. He was just so sweet.

"I'll just walk. It's only like a fifteen-minute walk. I'll be fine."

"Okay," Zen said. "See you tomorrow."

After an hour of folding the clothes that club members had finally dropped off, Apple walked home alone. She was lonely and felt awful about what she had slipped to Zen about Happy's lifeguard experience. Joggers and golf carts passed by her. She waved to George as she walked by, but she didn't stop, even as he called out, "Have a good night, Applesauce!"

Just as she was walking up her front door, her cell phone started to ring.

"Hey, Apple!"

It was Happy. She knew she was calling to find out if Apple had gotten any information out of Zen. Happy was all about instant gratification. She wanted answers ASAP. What was she going to tell Happy? That she had just made her out to seem like a party girl? That she was a bad friend?

"Thank you!" Happy screeched, before Apple could even say hello. "Thank you! Thank you! Thank you!"

"For what?" Apple asked, surprised.

"Zen! He asked me out to a movie on Friday," Happy shrieked.

"He *did*?" Apple asked, mystified.

"Yes, whatever you said to him, thank you! I owe you big time!"

"No, you don't," Apple said, feeling baffled. Here she was, feeling so guilty about how she had portrayed Happy, and yet whatever she had said had made him ask her out. "So when did he ask you out? I mean, I'm just getting home now. I thought he was going home, because he said he wasn't feeling well. I guess he wasn't too sick to call you."

"He asked me out after school today. I wanted to call you earlier, but I had an appointment with Dr. Caffeine and had to race out of school. I just got home.

I thought you were going to wait to talk to him while you were do-gooding, but I guess you spoke to him at school today, right?" Happy pressed.

"Um, yeah," Apple said. Why hadn't Zen told her that he had already asked Happy out? And there she had been talking about Happy's lifeguard!

"Well, like I said, whatever you said, *thank you!* It totally worked. And I wasn't even thinking about getting a date out of this. I just wanted to know where his head was at, you know? But this is so much better!" Happy squealed.

"Um, no problem. Listen," Apple said. "I'm just walking in the door. I'll speak to you later."

"Thanks again, Apple. It really means the world to me. I couldn't ask for a better best friend," Happy said. "I owe you big . . . You may even get a pair of shoes along with those jeans!"

Apple felt sick to her stomach.

She opened her front door, and, like finding out your favorite show was in repeats, Aunt Hazel was there.

"I'm warning you, I'm in a rotten mood," she told her aunt.

"Rotten apple!" her aunt taunted her. "Rotten apple! Rotten apple!"

"Hardy-har," Apple said. "Like I haven't heard that one before. Why are *you* in such a good mood?"

"I've decided to go on strike," Aunt Hazel said. "I feel great about my decision."

"What are you talking about? From your job?" Apple asked, sitting down on the couch next to her.

"No. I've decided I'm going on strike from all men. I'm taking a break. No more men for me," Aunt Hazel said, decidedly.

"Right. That should last, like, an hour?" Apple said.

"Why are you in such a crabby mood?" her aunt asked. "I mean, shouldn't you be walking on cloud nine, with this huge crush of yours?"

Did her Crazy Aunt Hazel know about Zen? How could she know? Apple hadn't told anybody. She had never been more secretive.

"What are you talking about?" Apple asked hesitantly.

"Oh, nothing. Just a little bird told me that you were in love with an older man, that's all. And a teacher! You are such a bad girl, Apple. I never knew you had it in you. You'd better be careful or people are going to start calling you Bad Apple. But I'm impressed. So, is he that cute?"

Take cleansing breaths, like Brooklyn always suggested, Apple thought to herself. Unbelievable! Now her mother was telling her secret, her fake problem, to Crazy Aunt Hazel? Her mother really had no boundaries!

"You know Apple, he'll never go for you, no matter how cute you are," her aunt continued, when Apple didn't respond. "Do you really think he'd risk his job for a student? Sometimes it's better to just quit. Oh, I know everyone always tells you that you should never quit anything, except smoking. But in relationships, it's different. Sometimes—and trust me on this—it's better to let the one you love go. Why don't you quit Mr. Kelly and go on strike with me? Because it will never happen anyway."

"Leave me alone!" Apple screamed at her aunt, getting up from the couch. "Just leave me the hell alone."

Apple had no idea where that had come from. It had leapt out of her mouth before she could stop it. Apple was not usually a yeller.

"God, you need to take it easy. I'm going," her aunt huffed. "You know, maybe your mother is right. Maybe you should open up more—"

Apple didn't wait to hear the rest, and turned and ran upstairs.

EVERYTHING and EVERYONE was getting to her.

ten

a pple stormed upstairs from the back hallway to her mother's home office, furious that Aunt Hazel knew about her fake diary entry and that her mother had had the nerve to discuss it with her—Aunt Hazel! Of all people!

My mother thinks she can just read my private diary entries on my computer, thought Apple, with revulsion. Well, if it's all right for her to do it to *me*, then it must be all right for me to do it to *her*.

Apple clicked her mother's computer on, and entered the password to log in. Her mother was so unoriginal. Her password, Apple knew, was P-A-S-S-W-O-R-D. Apple had been around years ago when Guy had first explained to her mother about the computer and she knew her technophobic mother would never change it. Ever.

Up on the screen popped up dozens upon dozens of e-mails, with the subject line "Help Please!"—all meant for the eyes of Dr. Bee Bee Berg.

Was she really going to do this? Apple knew it was so immoral. Yet, at the same time, she felt like she needed to be reassured that others out there in the world were as miserable as she was. Of course, she also wanted to get back at her mother for reading her personal diary.

Randomly, Apple clicked and opened one of the e-mails.

Dear Queen of Hearts,
Is it so wrong to have sex with the ex? You're the only one who can understand me, and I want more than anything to be on your show. But let me tell you my problem. I broke up with my ex after a three-year relationship. We hadn't had any contact in two months, when we ran into each other at a party and I ended up going home with him. All the old feelings came rushing back. It's been over a week and I haven't heard from him. But I haven't called him either. I'm not saying I want to get back together. I know we're over. But how could it feel so right at the time, and not mean anything to him? Please give me your advice! I need your advice!

Apple felt a huge knot in her stomach. Reading another person's painful admission about her disappointments didn't exactly make her feel better about her own problems. It just made her feel worse—and gloomier than ever.

Once, years ago, Apple had come home to find a folder marked "Queen of Heart Shows" on the kitchen table, where Guy had left it. Apple had mindlessly picked it up, more because it was there than out of curiosity about what was in it. The folder had been full of letters sent by snail mail from viewers, writing to her mother, telling her their sordid love tales and explaining why they needed to go on her show.

Apple remembered being in the middle of a twelve-page, double-sided, single-spaced, handwritten letter from a woman telling her mother about her secret affair with her sister's fiancé. Apple had found herself thoroughly entranced with the story, not so much with what the writer was going through as with her openness in sharing it. And putting it on paper! Even at age ten, Apple knew way more about love than most adults, but because this woman and her sister and the fiancé were all willing to go on television and talk about it, she was astonished. She had just gotten to the part in the letter where the woman was saying that the fiancé was still choosing between the sisters when her mother and Guy had walked into the room.

"What do you think you're doing?" her mother had asked her as Guy raced over and grabbed the letter, giving her hand a little slap.

"Hey! I was just in the middle of that!" Apple had said, trying to grab the letter back from Guy, who was hiding it behind his back. "What's the big deal?"

"How would you feel," she remembered her mother asking, "if you knew someone was reading a personal letter *you* sent? And you're ten! How would you feel if you found out you sent someone a letter and a ten-year-old was reading it?"

"How would they ever find out?" Apple remembered having asked, and her mother had told her that that wasn't the point. "The point is that you have to respect people's privacy," she swore her mother had told her.

"Privacy? What a joke!" Apple had said. "They're asking to be on your show. They want to tell you their problems in front of so many people they don't even know!"

She remembered vaguely that her mother had looked over at Guy, and that Guy had shrugged his shoulders, as if to say, "You answer that." Apple had known her mother didn't know how to respond.

But again, her mother had told her that that wasn't the point. "They're writing to *me*," she had responded.

Obviously, her mother's views on privacy had changed, Apple thought sarcastically. Obviously, her mother now felt that it was okay to invade people's privacy, even those who were related to her by blood.

She clicked on another e-mail randomly. See how my mother likes *this*, Apple thought.

Dear Queen of Hearts,
How is it that two people can be on such different pages in the same relationship? I told someone who I was with for a while, and who I believed really loved me like I loved him, that if he asked me to marry him, I would say yes. He said it was never going to happen. That ended our relationship instantly. I'm feeling so rejected.

Suddenly, a subject line on one of the e-mails caught Apple's eye. It read, "Apple's friend needs help!!!"

This was curious, Apple thought, a little terrified to open it. But she did, holding her breath.

Dear Dr. Bee Bee Berg,
I know this is strange, me being the best friend of your daughter. It's me, Happy. I just really need some objective advice. And, it's like you always say, even your best friends just want you to be happy, so they won't tell you the truth. I have a date with this guy I really like on Friday night. It's the first time that I've really liked someone. And it's weird, because even though we've been going to the same school for years, I never really knew he existed. So I don't want to screw this up. I've never really been in a serious relationship. As I'm sure Apple has told you, I watch your show religiously, like she is obsessed with *Minors in Malibu*. So can you please tell me how I should act? Do you have any surefire ways of NOT screwing up a first date? I really appreciate you taking the time.
xoxox
Happy

Apple reread the e-mail a dozen times. How could Happy do this to her, and behind her back? She felt betrayed. After all, her friend felt comfortable enough asking her to find out information about how Zen was feeling about her. She felt comfortable enough asking her to put in a good word to Zen. She felt comfortable enough asking her how to get on *Queen of Hearts*. Why wasn't her best friend asking *her* for advice? Apple ran her hands through her mop of hair. Why was everyone who supposedly loved her disappointing her so much? Happy not telling Apple she was doing this stung almost as much as Plan Z bombing. Apple found herself hitting Reply. She told herself that she simply was not going to let her mother pass off her tired old advice on Happy. She, Apple, knew Happy better than anyone in the world, after all. Apple rubbed her hands together and started to type a response. You can do this, Apple. Just pretend you are a younger, more hip version of Dr. Bee Bee Berg. Just pretend you are your mother, giving out advice. You *are* the daughter of Dr. Bee Bee Berg. You must have it in you somewhere to dish it out. If Guy can do it, and he's a man, *you* can do it. Think, Apple, think.

"Dear Happy," she typed. "It's so nice to hear from you. I'm sorry I haven't seen more of you recently . . ."

Now what would her mother's advice be? She knew her advice would be to just be yourself. That was always her mother's no-nonsense advice to people when they worried about first dates or blind dates or meeting people on the Internet.

No, thought Apple. I need Happy and Zen's date *not* to work out. Because if it did, that could lead to a second date . . . and a third . . . and if it didn't work out between them after all that, then Apple would be caught in between her best friend and Zen. And then if they started hating each other, Apple would never even be able to talk to Zen again, because she would have to side with Happy. No, she had to stop Happy and Zen from starting anything significant. What would the opposite of her mother's advice be? That was what Apple had to send Happy. She had to send Happy bad advice, not good advice. Apple felt like a crazy person. She felt like Crazy Aunt Hazel must have felt, when she was caught by—what was his name?—sneaking through the stuff in his closet. She just couldn't stop herself. She realized, the more she thought about it, that she now, more than ever, wanted to be the one to go out on a date with Zen. She wished she was the one who was so worried about a first date. She thought of all the ways Aunt Hazel had screwed up on her dates. That would be perfect, Apple thought. She'd just send Happy tips to do the things that had always resulted in disaster for Hazel. She continued to type.

Here are three tips you should absolutely follow on a first date. One, flirt mercilessly, and look your very sexiest. Put on some of your best perfume and be sassy. Touch him. Two, compliment him mercilessly. Flattery will get you everywhere. Keep telling him how great he is. Three, find out as much about his interests as you can, even if this means looking through his address book on his phone. And the most important tip: don't act all that emotionally involved or interested. I know this sounds weird, but people are

always attracted to what they can't have. So
act like he can't have you. I think that's it for
now. Good luck on your date, and let me
know how it all works out.
Dr. Bee Bee Berg

Apple reread what she had written. She knew she
had just advised Happy to do what had always failed
for her aunt when she was in relationships or dating
someone. And also, from the brief conversation she had
with Zen at the club, she knew she was telling Happy
to act in a way Zen would detest, or that would at the
very least make him uncomfortable. Zen would
absolutely hate it if Happy flattered him too much.
Apple knew this.

Apple hated herself. No, she wouldn't send it. How
could she? She was not an evil person. She was just confused about everything. And just writing it out had made
her feel better anyway. She was about to delete her
response when she heard footsteps coming up the stairs.

Apple immediately felt her heart speed up.

"H-e-l-l-o? Anybody up here?" she heard Guy call out.

She raced to close down the computer. But her
fingers couldn't keep up with her racing mind. All she
could think about was that Guy was here and he was
going to catch her. She ran her fingers over the mouse
pad. Why, thought Apple, is this computer taking so
long to do anything? She started clicking away like a
madwoman, paying more attention to the sound of
Guy's footsteps than to what she was doing. Shut
down, computer! Shut down!

Your message has been successfully sent. The message suddenly popped up on the screen. My message has been what? WHAT?

Oh my God, Apple thought when she realized what she had done. She had sent the e-mail to Happy! In her panic trying to log out and not get caught, she had sent out her response e-mail.

"Apple!" Guy said, just as Apple shut down her mother's computer. Thank God, the screen had gone black.

"Oh, hey, Guy," she said, her heart pounding a million times a second. Apple was sure her face was as red as a fire truck. Still, she swiveled around in the chair to face him, trying to act as normally as possible in this state of disaster.

"What are you doing up here?" he asked.

"Oh, well, um, my computer is having troubles and I had to send in a class assignment, so I had no choice but to use this one. I've just finished. So it's all yours," Apple said.

"Thanks, darling!" Guy said. "Guy's got a ton to do. There's no rest for the wicked!"

"Where's Mom tonight?" Apple asked, still trying to act like she hadn't just made the biggest mistake of her life.

"She's accepting the city's Woman of the Year Award," Guy said.

"Didn't she already get that?" Apple asked. She scanned her eyes over the walls, which were covered in framed awards.

"Well, yes. But it seems they have Woman of the Year awards almost every week!" Guy laughed. "I wonder where she'll hang this one? You know, you guys may have to move to a bigger place to hang all of her awards."

"Well, I've got more schoolwork to do," Apple said, "See ya!" She headed up to her room.

What had she done? How was it possible for her to make so many wrong turns in one day? There was nothing for Apple to do now but wait. Wait to see if Zen broke his date with Happy. And, if he didn't, wait to see if Happy followed her awful advice. She also had to wait to see if she would get caught having snuck into her mother's e-mail. And, worst of all, she would have to wait to see, if the date did in fact happen, if it turned out to be a good date, where the conversation flowed effortlessly, they made each other laugh, and, gulp, they couldn't keep their hands off each other.

eleven

𝒶 t 10 p.m. on Friday night, Apple found herself sitting next to Brooklyn on a beanbag chair at Club Rox. Guy had driven her there, after dropping by the house to pick up some work. Apple had had butterflies in her stomach all week. For most of the week, in fact, she had felt like lying under her covers in bed and never coming out. And now that it was Friday, she was in pure obsession mode. It was good for her to be out, she thought. It was good that Zen hadn't seemed to tell Happy about her telling him about the lifeguard fling. At least, Apple thought, being out with Brooklyn will hopefully help me keep my mind off Zen and Happy, who are on their date right now. The club was packed, teeming with students. Her mother had some event that night, and her dad had gone to the club with some of his co-workers. God only knew where Aunt Hazel was. Or with whom.

Apple sipped on a rum and Coke, thanks to Brooklyn's foresight. They had poured it into their Cokes under the table. Apple was impressed. Not only had Brooklyn managed to sneak out of her house from under the watchful eyes of the Helicopter, she had managed to steal a bottle of rum on her way out. It was exactly what Apple needed. She wasn't a drinker, but she wanted to at least try to shut her brain off. She wanted to try to have fun. And if she had to get drunk to do it . . .

Apple couldn't help but think, at that point, that Happy and Zen had been on their date for almost two hours. She looked at her watch. Yup. Two and a half hours now.

"I bet it's going well," Brooklyn said. "Don't you think it is?"

Apple knew Brooklyn was talking about Happy and Zen's date. Like her mother, Brooklyn was always optimistic about love.

"Probably," Apple answered. "What could go wrong?"

"Right! It's Happy after all. Everything always works out for Happy," Brooklyn said. "She puts out good vibes into the world." It was all Apple could do to grunt out a response. She was here to have fun and keep her mind off The Date, not here to talk about it all night.

"So, see any cute boys?" Apple asked Brooklyn, scanning the room, trying to get out of the conversation.

"I see a few," Brooklyn answered, nodding her head toward a guy standing by a wall alone. "What do you think about him?"

"Not my type," Apple answered. "He's wearing a tie-dyed T-shirt. I think he's way more your type, Brooklyn."

She knew her only *type* was Zen, but she couldn't exactly say that to Brooklyn. She didn't even know why she had such a huge crush on him and had for so long. She just knew that she did. Apple didn't think she could ever be attracted to a guy who wasn't Zen. She had invested so much time into liking Zen and obsessing about him from afar that she hadn't even thought about other guys in years.

"Brooklyn, I think that guy is staring at you right now," Apple said. "And it looks kind of like he has a yoga body, too."

"Where? Where?" Brooklyn asked.

"That guy you pointed out standing alone by the wall!" Apple said, and Brooklyn slyly looked over.

"He's kind of cute, isn't he?" Brooklyn asked, after furtively checking him out again while pretending to look for someone she knew in the club.

"He is," Apple agreed.

"I think he's checking *you* out, not me," Brooklyn said.

"Um, no. He's definitely checking *you* out. You should go talk to him," Apple suggested.

"No, I can't leave you. Hey, I think I hear your phone ringing," Brooklyn said. "It's definitely not mine. Remember? The Helicopter took it away."

Apple looked into her bag, which was on a low table in front of them. Brooklyn bopped her head to the loud music.

"Hello?" Apple yelled over the noise, holding a hand over her other ear. "Happy? Is that you?"

"Yes, it's me! Are you guys still out? Where are you? At Rox? I can barely hear you. I'm coming to meet you guys now," she heard Happy say.

"What?" Apple screamed.

"I SAID I'M COMING TO MEET YOU!" Happy screamed into her ear. "I'll be there in about twenty minutes. Sailor's just leaving the house now, so she'll drop me off. See you soon!"

Apple closed her phone and put it back into her bag.

"That was Happy?" Brooklyn asked.

"Yup. She's coming to meet us," Apple said, taking a long sip of her drink. When had she become so nervous about seeing her best friend?

"Cool! Wait. It's only twenty to eleven." Brooklyn said, looking at her watch. "Do you think that means her date was crappy or something?"

"I don't know," Apple said. "I guess we'll find out soon."

"Oh, God. I really hope it didn't go badly. I really think Happy likes him. I hope she's okay," Brooklyn said, twisting her hair around her fingers viciously. It was what Brooklyn did when she was nervous and there were no yoga mats around.

"I'm sure she's fine. It's Happy! Happy never has a bad time," Apple said, trying to sound convincing. "Like you said, she has good vibes."

"You're right. You're right. She'll be here soon and will tell us everything."

Almost exactly twenty minutes later, they saw Happy saunter in. Apple couldn't help but notice all the guys studying her as she walked by them. That was the effect Happy's look had on strangers. She was like Moses parting the Red Sea.

"Hey!" Happy said, lightheartedly, taking a seat on the beanbag. "This place is crazy! Apple, you look pretty. Hey, are you drunk?" Happy asked. "Your eyes are so red."

"Thanks. And, yes, I think I may be a little drunk. So, how did the date go? Where did he take you? What did you guys do? Did you have fun?" Apple asked, hating herself for sounding so, well, so much like her nosy mother.

"It was fine," Happy said. "It was fun. We had a good time."

"Fine? Fine? What does 'fine' mean?" Brooklyn pressed.

"It was fine, that's what I mean. It was fine," Happy repeated, shrugging her shoulders.

Brooklyn and Apple exchanged looks. Usually Happy was so open and willing to talk about the details of every aspect of her life. Happy was like the guests on *Queen of Hearts with Dr. Bee Bee Berg*. She had no problem sharing the most intimate details of her life, especially not with her two best friends. She even liked shocking her friends with her antics.

"Come on, guys! Don't look at each other like that," Happy said. "I'm sitting right here! I can see you!"

"Okay," said Apple carefully. "So what exactly did you guys do?"

"We went to dinner and walked around and went for a coffee," Happy said. "God, the music is rocking tonight. Anyone up for some dancing? Because I know I am."

"Wait," Apple said, grabbing her friend's arm. Happy had stood up, ready to hit the dance floor. "So was dinner good?"

She knew, from being a private person herself, when someone didn't want to talk, and yet she couldn't stop pressing Happy for information. She felt the way she imagined her mother must feel when she pressed Apple for answers. It was frustrating not to get answers, especially detailed answers.

"It was fine, like I said," Happy responded, starting to shake her hips to the beat of the music.

Apple knew the date with Zen couldn't have been that good if all Happy would say was that it was "fine." Fine was not good. She knew that something must have gone wrong, and that Happy didn't want to talk about it. She wondered if Happy had followed her advice and had spent dinner complimenting and flattering Zen, something Apple knew made him very uncomfortable. She wondered if Happy had made a fool of herself by "flirting mercilessly" like she had suggested while pretending to be Dr. Bee Bee Berg responding to Happy's e-mail.

"I'm going to the dance floor," Happy said. "Are you guys coming with me or not? I just feel the need to dance."

"I'm in," said Brooklyn. "This guy has been checking me out, and I think he may follow us."

"I think I'm going to go home, actually," Apple said. She felt so woozy suddenly that she wondered if it was going to be possible for her stand up, let alone dance.

"Don't go! I just got here," Happy said, pouting at her friend and grabbing her arm. "Let's dance! Sailor told me the Fire Room is so freaking cool, all painted in flames. We should go check it out. And then we'll go to the Ice Room, where they have these huge ice sculptures."

"No, I think I really am coming down with something. I feel a bit woozy. I should go and get some rest," Apple said.

"That's the rum talking. You drank quite a bit, you know," Brooklyn said.

"Yeah, silly," Happy said, laughing. "You're drunk!"

"Well, drunk or not, I'm not feeling great. So I'm going to head home. But you guys stay. Stay and have a good time! I have to go out and help with the clothing drive tomorrow, and I should sleep this off." She could hear herself slurring her words. "Hey, Happy. You want me to ask Zen anything for you? He'll be there tomorrow too."

I'm definitely drunk, Apple thought. She had gone from not wanting to meddle in anyone's life to actually offering to meddle.

"Nah, that's okay. Oh, but Apple?" Happy said, grabbing Apple's hand.

"Yeah?" Apple asked. Maybe now Happy was going to tell her what had really happened on the date. That it had been a total failure and that she felt like an idiot for thinking she might ever really like Zen.

"There's something you should know," Happy said. "Do you think you'll remember what I tell you now, or should I wait for tomorrow?"

"Don't be ridiculous, Happy! I'm not *that* drunk!"

Apple instantly felt paranoid. Did Zen mention to Happy on their date what Apple had told him about Happy's fling with the lifeguard?

"Just tell me," Apple pressed.

"I wrote an e-mail to your mother asking her for advice," Happy said.

Oh, Apple thought. Phew. Happy *didn't* know that she had told Zen about the lifeguard. "Why? And when?" she asked, even though she knew the answer.

"When I got home tonight. I just thought you should know, since I know how much you hate that I think she's good at giving out advice," Happy said, looking slightly guilty.

"Just tonight? After your date?" Apple asked, bewildered.

"Yeah, to tell you the truth, I'm not that confident the date was all that great. So I really needed an expert's opinion. I hope you don't mind," Happy said. "It just seemed like such an easy thing to do. And she is an expert, after all. And I didn't want to ask you again, to ask Zen about it. You've already done so much for me."

"No, I don't mind," Apple told her friend. "If you think it will make you feel better."

"Thanks, Apple, for understanding," Happy said appreciatively, giving Apple a huge hug.

Happy's date must have really gone awry if she felt it necessary to go to Apple's mother for advice—again.

"I understand. So why aren't you confident?" Apple asked Happy, with concern. "It couldn't have been that bad."

"I don't want to discuss it here. Some other time I'll tell you. For now I just want to dance. Let's go, Brooklyn."

Apple hugged her two friends goodbye. She was shocked to realize that she was smiling as she walked out of Club Rox. She got into a cab that was waiting out front and gave the driver her address.

Maybe Zen wasn't that into Happy after all, she thought. Maybe they realized that beyond their initial attraction, they had nothing in common.

She couldn't help but wonder what Happy had written to her mother, though. No, thought Apple, I must resist the temptation. I'm never going to sneak into my mother's personal e-mail again, even if she did it to me first. I'm not that person, Apple thought to herself. I believe in a person's right to privacy. Happy would tell her what happened eventually, probably even the next day. Happy wasn't the one who kept secrets and feelings to herself. That was Apple's role.

Apple rolled down the taxi's windows. The cool air was making her feel better. She looked out and saw the stars. Maybe life wasn't that bad after all. Maybe it had just been a bad couple of weeks and now things would get back to normal and Zen would realize that the one he should have asked on the date was Apple.

As soon as she walked into her house, Apple knew she needed a distraction from her mother's computer, which seemed to be calling out to her, "Log on! Log on!" She swore she could hear it whispering to her. No, I will not log on, she told herself. She thought she had clearly made up her mind during the taxi ride home, but it was as if she couldn't make the decision stick.

She headed up to her room, noticing, for what seemed like the zillionth time, that the doors to both the spare bedroom and her parents' bedroom were closed—which meant that, once again, her parents weren't sleeping together in the same room. Apple wasn't an expert on relationships, but it didn't take a genius or a relationship expert to know there were marital problems in the Berg household, she thought. What if people found out that the woman who dished out relationship advice knew that her own relationship at home was a wreck?

She wondered if she had missed another blowout this evening. But her parents' issues were not hers, Apple thought. Whatever was going on between them was between *them*. They were adults and should know how to figure their own issues out. She had her own problems. At that moment, her biggest problem seemed to be how she was going to force herself *not* to log on to her mother's computer, to check out what Happy had written to Dr. Bee Bee Berg after her date that night with Zen.

She wandered into the kitchen. I'll just make myself a snack, she thought, taking a box of cereal out of the cupboard. She took out a bowl and spoon and got the milk from the fridge.

Five minutes later, she was done. Now what? she thought. Her mind kept wandering to what Happy possibly had written. No, I'm not going to look, thought Apple. If Happy wanted to tell me what happened on her date, she would have. If she wanted to know what I thought, she would have asked me. I'm just going to go up and get ready for bed and go to sleep.

Twenty minutes after getting into bed, Apple knew it was fruitless to try and fall asleep. Her body was tired, but her mind was going wild.

Maybe it wouldn't be that big a deal just to read what Happy had written. No one would ever find out, she thought. And Happy would probably tell her everything later anyway. No, I can't, Apple thought. I can't and I won't. Her parents' issues were not hers, and neither were Happy's. And that was that.

She found herself saying to herself, "I can't and I won't," even as she snuck by her parents' room to make sure her mother was sleeping, and as she snuck by the spare bedroom to hear the sound of her father's rhythmic snoring.

I can't and I won't, she thought as she tiptoed down the hallway into her mother's office.

"How can I be doing this?" she asked out loud as she turned on her mother's computer and waited for it to boot up.

She bit on one of her fingernails. What kind of person am I turning into? she thought. Apple wasn't the nail-biter. Brooklyn was.

You are so mean, Apple thought to herself. Then, no, you're not. You're concerned about your friend. And you're not going to fall asleep until you look at it anyway, so if you want to get at least a couple hours of sleep before volunteering tomorrow, you might as well just do it. It was normal to be interested in a friend's problem. She was justified to be concerned.

She walked back to the doorway to listen for any new sounds of movement from her parents' room. She couldn't hear anything and headed back to the computer.

P-A-S-S-W-O-R-D, she typed quickly. Apple thought if she did this fast enough, it would be over, like pulling off a Band-Aid.

She still felt tipsy from the rum she had drunk at Club Rox. Could she blame what she was doing on liquid courage? That was reasonable. Sort of.

The subject line caught her eye immediately. She knew it was Happy's e-mail. It read, "Advice needed from Apple's friend . . . again."

So there it was—the e-mail that Happy had told Apple she had sent to her mother after her date.

Apple knew it wasn't too late. She could log off, shut down the computer now, go back to her room, and just try to fall asleep. Or even just lay there not falling asleep. She still had the choice to read it or not. Apple knew this. But her head was telling her one thing, and her heart another.

Just like when she was ten, and her mother and Guy had caught her reading her mother's mail, she found herself asking, "What's the big deal?" And she followed her heart.

She clicked on the e-mail Happy had sent and read it, feeling a knot in her stomach as big as a watermelon. Maybe she shouldn't have eaten that bowl of cereal. Cereal and rum just did not mix.

Dear Dr. Berg,
Thanks for your quick reply to my first e-mail. And thank you so much for giving me that advice. I have to admit that I didn't follow all of it, but some of it, I think, worked. It's hard to tell. Which is why I need your advice—again. Zen—that's his name—didn't seem exactly himself tonight. It seemed like there was

something he wanted to ask me the whole
night but couldn't quite get out. I don't know.
Maybe it was first-date jitters or something.
What do you think? The conversation went
pretty well. But then, at the end of the night,
when he walked me home, I think he wanted
me to invite him in. I wanted to, but at the
same time I also wanted the night to end,
without there being some big finale. You know
what I mean. It's like when you're having a
great time at a party and you want to leave
before you know it gets bad. That was what it
was like. I didn't want to get sick of him. Or I
didn't want him to get sick of me. I don't
know. But when I said goodnight, he leaned in
and we kissed! And it was amazing! It lasted
like five minutes. I didn't want it to end, but,
again, like a good party, I wanted it to stop,
while I was still having fun. It's hard to explain.
And then, after, it was a little awkward, I'll
admit, because it did seem like there was still
something he wanted to ask me . . . Am I
being paranoid, Dr. Berg?
xoxox
Happy

Apple suddenly knew she had to get up. She ran to
the washroom attached to her mother's office. She
knew she was about to be sick. Really sick. She made
it to the toilet just in time and held back her hair with
one hand while she threw up. She tried to gag as quietly

as possible. Sweat poured from her forehead. I am never going to drink again, Apple told herself. She suddenly had a pounding headache. How could this have happened? she thought, blinking back tears. She wiped her eyes and her face. She flushed the toilet. She rinsed out her mouth, splashed cold water on her face, and, unsteadily, started walking back to her mother's computer, tripping over a garbage can on the way. Why didn't Happy tell her and Brooklyn about the kiss? Why did she say that she wasn't confident about the date, when they had ended up kissing? Happy and Zen kissed. Happy and Zen kissed. Happy and Zen kissed. Happy and Zen kissed!

Apple clicked Reply. The room was spinning and she had to force herself to concentrate on the letters on the keyboard. Focus, Apple, focus.

Dear Happy,
Thank you for keeping me updated. I hate to tell you this, but I think you may not be wrong in your feeling about being paranoid. Two things: if he seemed like he was trying to ask you something, it could have been that he is hiding something. This is never a good sign, especially at the start of a relationship. That's just something for you to consider. I'm not saying I'm right, but just that it's something for you to consider. Second, chemistry is a good thing, but it's not everything. A good kiss could mean just that Zen is a good kisser, and nothing more. That's something else for you to

consider. If I were you, I'd play "hard to get" now. But, of course, I leave it up to you.
Dr. Bee Bee Berg

Apple reread what she had written, paying very close attention to each word. She knew she wasn't exactly seeing straight, and it was hard to type without making spelling mistakes. Her mother and Guy never made spelling mistakes in their responses. Spelling was their pet peeve. This time Apple didn't think twice about clicking Send. She shut down her mother's computer and headed back to her bedroom. Now she was exhausted—emotionally, physically, and mentally. She plopped herself down on her bed, shivering under the covers. She just couldn't keep warm. Her head still pounded and the tears kept springing to her eyes. Her mother was right—never underestimate what heartbreak can do to a girl, she always advised her viewers. Apple was drunk and miserable. She hated herself for sending out that e-mail without even a second thought, as if Happy deserved it. She also hated feeling like she had been run over by a truck.

Apple closed her eyes and passed out.

twelve

It was Saturday morning. Apple had woken up after a fitful sleep to a pounding head and to the image of Zen and Happy kissing. She couldn't get them out of her head, like a horrible verse in a pop song. She groaned out loud when she remembered what she had done when she had got home. She should never drink again. The problem with drinking to forget is that you wake up and remember. And there could be nothing worse than drinking and e-mailing. She painfully got out from under her covers, feeling overwhelmed with nausea, partly because of the alcohol she had consumed, but mostly because of the thought of Happy and Zen kissing. You had a Girl Crazy Moment sending that e-mail out to Happy, like Aunt Hazel did when she thought it would be wise to sneak a peek in that guy's house after she had spent the night. It was *just* a Girl Crazy Moment, and it will *never* happen again. You will never enter Girl Crazy Territory ever again like that, Apple told herself. If anyone should know better, it should be Apple.

You have to get your shit together now, thought Apple.

Though she felt like staying in bed all day, she knew she couldn't. Zen and his mother were driving over in half an hour to pick Apple up on the way to the club.

She ran her tongue over her teeth and felt a thin disgusting layer. She decided to shower, taking her toothbrush in with her. After she toweled off, she walked to her closet and stood inside, looking at all her clothes. Her brain was so frizzled that it took her almost twenty minutes to decide what to put on. What outfit had Zen not seen her in? She felt like crap, but she couldn't look like crap. Not in front of Zen. She chose a simple, tight black T-shirt and a pair of skinny jeans from Happy and swiped on some lip gloss.

The doorbell rang, and Apple ran downstairs.

"Hey, you ready?" Zen asked when Apple opened the door.

His mother waved to Apple from the car.

"As ready as I'll ever be today," she answered. She couldn't look him in the eye. All she could picture in her head was his lips on Happy's last night, and it was making her feel sick all over again.

"Wow. Apple, you look really tired," Zen said.

"Thanks," Apple said.

"You know what I mean. Did you have a late night?" Zen asked.

"Yeah. Sort of," Apple said, grabbing her bag and shutting the door behind them as they walked to Zen's mother's car.

"You partied, didn't you?" Zen said. "Admit it. I can tell. You literally look green."

"A bit," she admitted.

Apple didn't know how she made it through the eight-minute drive to get to the club. Zen's mother was asking her all about Dr. Bee Bee Berg, and telling Apple she had seen her mother's photo in the newspaper again, and that she would love to invite Apple and Dr. Berg over for dinner one night. Apple didn't say much. She couldn't. She was scared that if she opened her mouth, she would end up puking.

Finally, after what seemed like an hour, Zen's mother dropped them off and they headed to their post inside the club.

They sat at their table, watching the golf and tennis fanatics walk by. A few people dropped off boxes of clothes on their way to brunch.

"So, aren't you going to ask what I did last night?" Zen asked suddenly.

Apple looked at him, picking her head off the table. She wasn't sure how to respond.

"What did you do last night?" she asked him, robotically. Her voice sounded monotone. I already know what you did, she screamed in her head miserably. You kissed Happy! You kissed my best friend!

"I went on a date with your friend Happy," Zen said, smiling with that dimple.

"Yeah, I know," said Apple, trying to not sound as drained as she felt.

"Right. Of course you know. You guys are best friends. I keep forgetting," Zen said. This annoyed

Apple. Why couldn't Zen even remember that Apple was Happy's best friend? Was Apple *that* forgettable?

"Yeah, she told us at Club Rox," Apple said.

"Wait. Happy went to Club Rox last night? What time?" Zen asked, sounding a little impatient.

"I don't know. Maybe eleven," Apple said, folding some clothes that had just been dropped off, and organizing them into different boxes. It was amazing what people were giving away. Some of the clothes still had the price tags hanging off of them.

Apple was so fatigued from not sleeping that she didn't realize until after she'd said it that Happy might not have wanted Zen to know she went out after their date. She tried quickly to cover her tracks, feeling guilt-ridden again over the e-mail she had sent to Happy, pretending to be Dr. Berg for a second time.

"She met us. But Brooklyn and I dragged her out," Apple said defensively. "It wasn't like she planned on meeting us or anything."

"So, what did you guys do there?" Zen asked, picking up a red cashmere sweater and attempting to fold it.

"We drank. We danced. Well, actually, Brooklyn and Happy danced. I left earlier than them. But when I was leaving, they were hitting the dance floor."

"She was out dancing?" Zen said, more as a statement than as a question.

"Yes—I mean, *no!* I mean, I don't know," Apple said. She didn't want to be put into the position of tattling on Happy again. Why did all their conversations have to center on Happy? "Can we talk about something else than Club Rox? The mere thought of it is making me feel sick," Apple moaned, wrapping her arms around her stomach.

"Sure," said Zen, sounding tense. "What do you want to talk about?"

"Let's talk about television," she said. "That will get my mind off my pounding head. Did you see the latest episode of *Minors in Malibu*? I love that show. What is your favorite show?" It was a lame question, she knew, but she didn't want to think anymore about Happy, or the kiss, or what finding out about her friend's kiss had made Apple herself do.

"Actually, I don't watch television," Zen said.

Apple was astonished. She had never met anyone who didn't watch television, or at least not who actually admitted to never watching television.

"You don't watch television? How can you not watch television?" asked Apple, dropping the clothes that were in her arms on the table in shock.

"Well, I watch football and basketball and occasionally car racing, but that's about it, really. I don't watch anything else," he said, with an apologetic shrug.

"Really?" asked Apple, still amazed. "You don't watch any other television—not even *Minors in Malibu*?"

"Minors in what?" Zen asked, perplexed.

"You've never even heard of *Minors in Malibu*? It's only like the top-rated drama Tuesday nights at nine!" Apple exclaimed. "It's only my all-time favorite show!"

"Nope. Never heard of it," Zen said.

"Well, I guess it *is* more of a girl thing," Apple said.

"I guess so," Zen answered.

What else didn't she know about her soulmate? Obviously, they would never be cuddling up on the couch watching *Minors in Malibu*, Apple thought dejectedly.

"Well, what about books?" Apple asked. "Do you like to read?"

"You know, car magazines," Zen answered. He pulled one out of his knapsack and started to flip through the pages, then stopped and pointed to a page. "Check out this engine."

Apple didn't know how to respond. She didn't care about cars. She barely liked to be in them. She would walk everywhere if she could. She wasn't even excited to be taking driving lessons soon.

"Well, what's your favorite school subject?" Apple asked, feeling pathetic. It was the same way she felt when people talked about the weather. You only talked about school out of school when you had nothing else to talk about. She just wanted—needed—something to talk about with Zen that had nothing to do with Happy.

"Science," he said.

"Really," Apple said. Science was her least favorite subject. She hated science.

"Really," he said, smiling at her. Oh, God, why does he have to have such a nice smile? she thought. Why does he have to have *that* dimple? It instantly brought on a wave of sadness. She remembered why she had fallen in love with him two years earlier. So what if Zen didn't watch television and if his favorite subject was science? He had a great smile and a good heart, and he was sweet.

"Can I ask you one more thing about last night?" Zen asked. "And about Happy?"

"Sure," Apple said, adding under her breath, "As if I could stop you."

How did they get here? Apple wondered to herself. She always thought Zen wasn't a talker, but now all he seemed to want to do was talk. And not just talk, but talk about Happy.

"Did Happy seem to be having a good time?" he asked.

"Happy always has a good time," Apple answered, leaning back in her chair.

"Oh," Zen said, lowering his eyes back to his car magazine.

"You know what I mean. She's a free spirit." She knew what Zen was trying to get at.

"Right," he said.

"You know, I hate to do this to you. But I think I have to leave," Apple said, standing up suddenly. "I think what I need more than anything right now is to go home and take a nap."

"Yeah, I understand," said Zen. "Go home and drink a lot of water. That should make you feel better. Plus, you covered for me on that first day. I can handle it from here."

"Thanks, Zen. Bye," Apple said.

It took Apple forty-five minutes to walk the fifteen-minute walk home. She knew that eventually she would feel better, if she drank enough water and got some sleep. Well, at least physically. But would she feel better mentally and emotionally?

thirteen

$\mathcal{A}$pple noticed two things as soon as she walked into Cactus High on Monday morning. First she noticed that there were signs posted on walls everywhere for the annual Valentine Ball. The Valentine Ball was the most important social night at Cactus High. Only upper-grade students were invited to the Valentine Ball.

Ever since fifth grade, Apple had heard the stories. Girls ended up crying in the bathroom because someone else showed up in the same dress, couples broke up on the dance floor and then got together with other people the same night, students snuck in alcohol, and something was always stolen from the school. Happy's older sister, Sailor, had said that at her first Valentine Ball, three students got so drunk they passed out, had to be raced to the hospital, and were sus-pended. That, and Stella, one of the seventh-grade teachers, who had signed up to help chaperone, was caught being felt up by Grant, a music teacher. Mr. Kelly showed off his break-dancing skills, which was the joke of the rest of the school year.

The second thing Apple noticed was Happy and Zen, talking very close together by their lockers. They were so close, they must have been whispering.

Apple wondered if they were arguing about something and if Zen had told her what Apple had said at the country club. Happy had called Apple three times over the weekend, but Apple couldn't get herself to call her back. She told herself that it was because she was hungover. But Apple knew she just couldn't stand to listen to Happy talk about Zen. Apple stared at them. It didn't really seem like they were arguing, she thought. In fact, it seemed the exact opposite, like Zen was whispering sweet nothings in Happy's ear and Happy was eating it up. They were so close their shoulders were touching, and Apple swore she could see Zen bend in toward Happy's head to inhale her hair.

Apple headed to the spiral staircase, praying that Happy wouldn't see her. It didn't work.

"Hey, Apple," she heard Happy call out. "What's going on? Where have you been? I tried calling you at home, on your cell. Are you hiding from me?"

Happy seemed like she was in extremely good spirits. She caught up and put her arm though Apple's.

"No, sorry," Apple said. "Friday night killed me. I was pretty much a zombie the entire weekend."

"You are such a lightweight," Happy said, laughing. "Now, can you believe all this?" she continued, waving her arms in the air.

"All what?" Apple asked.

"The Valentine Ball!" Happy said to her. "Can you believe it's finally here? And that we get to go! I'm so excited! Remember what Sailor told us about it? Oh, and we'll definitely have to go to Gossip. We should make a plan. Are you in?"

"Absolutely," Apple said, happy to agree with Happy.

"Sailor says that the only thing worse than going to the Valentine Ball would be not going to the Valentine Ball," Happy continued.

"I understand *that* logic," Apple said, laughing in relief.

Clearly, Happy was not angry with her. She had not found out about what she had told Zen about her. It felt good to laugh with her best friend. It felt like it had been weeks since Apple had laughed at all.

"Got to go to class," Happy called out, just as Zen and Hopper walked up to them. "See you guys later!"

Apple noticed that she gave Zen a wink. Hopper followed her. Now Apple was standing there alone with Zen. She felt her heart beat. He looked liked he had something on his mind—he was biting the inside of his cheek, and seemed concerned.

"Is something wrong, Zen? You seem, I don't know, a little down or something. Is everything okay?" Apple asked, putting her hand on his arm.

"Can I tell you a secret?" Zen asked. "Are you good at keeping secrets?"

"Um, my friends call me the Sponge, just because I'm so good at keeping secrets," Apple told him, giving his arm a little squeeze to reassure him.

She suddenly felt brave. "Well, you know how you told me that Happy came to meet you guys at Club Rox after our date?" Zen began.

"Yeah?"

"Well, it really bothered me at the time," Zen said.

"I could tell," Apple said.

"It was that obvious, huh?" he asked.

"Kind of," she answered.

"Well, I didn't realize why it bothered me until I got home," Zen said, running a hand through his hair.

"You were jealous," Apple said. "You thought she was out having a great time without you, and you got jealous."

"Hey! I guess the apple really doesn't fall far from the tree. I guess you really *are* Dr. Bee Bee Berg's daughter," Zen said, sounding surprised, looking *at* her. "It took me hours to figure out what I was feeling. I guess you have your mother's intuition."

Apple rolled her eyes. "Well, I think pretty much anyone in the world could have figured that out," she said. "It's not rocket science or anything."

"Really? Anyway, it doesn't matter. Yes, I was jealous. But then I thought, why should I be jealous? I mean, she did agree to go on a date with me. We instant message each other almost nightly, or talk on the phone," Zen said, perking up. "She must like me at least enough not to tell me to bugger off."

"You guys talk that often?" Apple asked.

"Yeah. She didn't tell you?"

"Anyway. Go on," she said, with a bit of a wave.

"Well, I thought instead of just sitting back, I should really show her that I do like her. I shouldn't just sit back and be jealous. I should do something with that jealousy. So I've decided to step up my game," he told Apple.

"Step up your game. What do you mean exactly?" Apple asked. "And why are you telling me all this?"

"I don't know," he said. "Happy told me you were a really good listener. I guess it has something to do with knowing you're the daughter of a relationship expert. I feel like I can talk to you," Zen said, wiping his forehead. "I usually don't talk like this. It's not easy for me."

"I wouldn't call my mother an expert about relationships. She's just a talk-show host," muttered Apple. God, Zen looked good. He was wearing a plain gray T-shirt and jeans. Even when he obviously didn't try, he looked good.

"From what I understand from Happy, she's much more than that," Zen said.

"Anyway, what were you going to say?" Apple asked. She wasn't in the mood to listen to raves about her mother right now.

"Well, it's pretty clear that Happy can get any guy she wants. I mean, you already told me about the lifeguard. So, I guess I'm just saying, so what if she likes to go out and have a good time—I can be the one to show her a good time. Or at least I can try. And, yes, she does seem to be hot and cold with me, but I like a challenge. Hey, I'm a guy. What guy doesn't like a challenge?" Zen said, sounding like he's trying to convince himself.

"So what you're saying is that you're ready to compete. You have your game face on," Apple asked, deliberately using a sports term she's heard her father use before.

"Exactly. So thanks for letting me know about Club Rox. And please, don't tell Happy I said this to you. I'm going to ask her to the dance. Wait, of course you won't. The Sponge, right?"

"I won't. I promise," Apple said. She slyly added, "But are you sure that's such a good idea?"

"What do you mean?" he asked, looking surprised. "You think I shouldn't ask her?"

"No, it's not that. It's just that the posters just went up today. If you ask her today, she might think you're like, I don't know, obsessed, or overly eager, or desperate. My mother always says to my Crazy Aunt Hazel that people can smell when you're desperate. That's all I'm saying."

"Hmm. Well, I guess that's something to think about," Zen said, sounding unsure.

"Well, my mother *is* the expert," Apple said cheerfully.

"Thanks for being such a good listener," Zen said. "I'm glad I can talk to you about this. And I'll think about what you said."

Zen walked down the hall to class. Apple walked out the front doors. Like Hazel, she felt she needed a mental health day. There was no way she could face sitting in a classroom all day knowing that Zen had his own plan, like she had her Plan Z. On her way home, she replayed their conversation. On the one hand, Zen obviously felt comfortable talking to her, which was a good thing. But on the other hand, he seemed to be even more obsessed with Happy now, even after she had tried to talk him out of asking her to the dance.

Apple put the earplugs to her iPod in her ears and blasted the music so she could forget her conversation. She had already given bad advice to Happy, and now she was giving idiotic advice to Zen. And he had said he was going to consider it!

She was also, much to her dismay, curious to see if Happy had written to her mother again. It was becoming an addiction, and not in a good way, thought Apple, as she let herself in the house. She slammed the door loudly, threw down her backpack, took off her iPod, and started up the stairs.

"Apple? Is that you? What are you doing home?" came a voice from somewhere upstairs.

"Mom?" asked Apple.

"Yes, dear. Who else would be up here?" her mother answered.

Apple hadn't planned on her mother being home at this hour, and she was disappointed. She had been anticipating going to her mother's office and finding out if there was another e-mail from Happy.

"I was listening to my iPod. I didn't hear anything," she told her mother, from where she still stood on the stairway.

"What are you doing home?" her mother asked. "Come up here."

Apple walked slowly up the rest of the stairs to her mother's office. Her legs felt heavy.

"Oh, you know, I wasn't feeling well and, well, I have a headache," Apple said. "And I think I may have a fever."

Her mother looked at her strangely. Apple knew her mother was contemplating whether she was lying. "I was just coming up because I saw the light on," Apple tried to explain. "Then I was going to go back down to lie down."

"Did you want to talk to me about something?" her mother asked, giving her a Dr. Bee Bee Berg look. It was a look that said, "You can tell me anything and I'll understand."

Apple didn't know how to respond. It had been so long since she had opened up to her mother, or to anyone for that matter. She wouldn't even know where to begin. She realized that she did want to confess everything that she had done, and what had been happening, but she was still angry with her mother for having read her personal diary.

"Oh, no," Apple said. "Like I said, I just saw the light on and was coming up to turn it off. What are you doing here all by yourself, anyway? Where's Guy?" Apple asked, scanning the room.

"Oh, I thought I was old enough to try to learn to log on myself. And guess what?" her mother asked, looking proud.

"What?" Apple asked.

"I figured it out! Well, there seem to be a few things I'm not understanding about this computer. But I've managed to log on and answer a few of the viewers' e-mails all by myself," her mother said, giddily. "I'm a modern woman!"

"That's great, Mom," Apple said, feeling her heart sink. There was no way her mother was computer-literate enough to see that Apple had sent out some e-mails, was there?

"Sit with me," her mother said, patting a spare chair beside her. "I feel like I don't ever see you anymore. I feel like we never have a chance to talk."

"Well, I don't have anything to talk about. Nothing new. Just school," Apple said, sitting upright on the edge of the chair.

"Well, Apple. Maybe you can help me out, then, with a little problem I seem to be having. I just received this e-mail from your friend Happy. I feel badly for her, because for some reason she thinks that I told her she should act emotionally unavailable to get a guy to really like her. Do girls your age really think that way? Do they really think that they must act all aloof to get a boy to notice them? And why would I ever tell that to any woman, let alone Happy?"

"I don't know," Apple said, gulping and pretending to pick a piece of lint of her pants.

"Well, it's an awful way to think. Playing games never got anyone very far, like I wrote in my book, *Stop the Games!* Because games always end. Or they never end, and you're in a crappy relationship for years," Dr. Bee Bee Berg said. She turned to her daughter. "You know that, right, Apple?"

"Yes, I know, Mom," she said.

"Good," Dr. Bee Bee Berg said. She looked back to the screen and shook her head. "I just don't understand how Happy could think that I would ever say something like that."

"What else did Happy write?" Apple asked.

"She seems to like a boy—one her age, mind you," Apple's mother said pointedly. God, her mother still thought she was in love with Mr. Kelly, her math teacher. She wasn't going to let Apple forget it. "And she was somehow under the impression that games were a good way to proceed," her mother finished.

"Well, what did you tell her?" Apple asked. "Did you write back?"

"You know, Apple, it gives me such joy when you're interested in my work. It really does," her mother gushed. "I honestly thought that you never cared about my work—or at least that you haven't for ages."

"Mom, just tell me what advice you gave her," Apple said.

"Well, I set her straight, of course," her mother answered firmly.

"You did?" Apple felt her heart sink. She tilted her head back and looked at the ceiling. She couldn't bring herself to look at her mother.

"Of course! I told her exactly what I just told you: that if you start playing games, then the games will end badly, or they will never end." Her mother paused and looked at Apple with concern. "You look pale, Apple. What's wrong? Maybe you *are* coming down with something."

"No, I'm just thinking about what Happy wrote you, that's all," Apple said quietly. She wasn't lying entirely. She *was* thinking about it. Plan Z had completely fallen apart. Now Happy would get the real Dr. Bee Bee Berg e-mail and think her mother was crazy for changing her tune and writing her completely different advice from what she seemed to have originally sent.

But there was still a chance that it would all be okay, if Happy thought Dr. Berg was a bit psychotic. Maybe Happy would even stop worshipping Dr. Bee Bee Berg so much—an added bonus, at least to Apple.

"I think I may have to have a little chat with Guy," her mother sighed. "I'm dreading it. You know how much he means to me. The Queen of Hearts would be nothing without Guy."

"Why do you have to have a chat with Guy?" Apple asked, now looking at her mother.

"You know he's usually the one who answers the viewer's e-mail questions. I just hope he isn't giving out bad advice. It's so strange, because he knows me like the back of his own hand. He knows I would never advise playing games. It's just so strange. Maybe he's overworked. Maybe I should give him some time off."

"Oh, I'm sure Guy didn't make a mistake," Apple swallowed. It felt like there was a huge lump stuck in her throat. "I'm sure Happy just got mixed up with advice she got from someone else. When people have problems, they usually ask everyone they know for advice, right?"

"You're probably right. She probably did get my advice mixed up with something her sister told her, or another one of her friends," her mother said, turning back to face the computer.

If only her mother knew how close to the truth that was, thought Apple.

Apple was done with sneaking into her mother's computer and checking to see if Happy had written to her. Done, done, done. This was *way* too close for comfort.

"Apple, I'm so happy we had this chat," her mother said, throwing her arms around her daughter. Apple didn't hug her back. "We should really do it more often," her mother added, letting her go. "But you really should go lie down. You look kind of green."

fourteen

$\mathcal{A}$pple and Zen were sitting behind their table at the country club folding clothes. Apple was in good spirits. She had made up her mind the day before, after speaking with her mother, to get back on the honest track, and it made her feel moral and sane again.

"It's pretty silly how the vibe in the school has changed in the past couple days," Zen said, putting his feet up on the table in front of him and taking a swig from his can of Coke.

"What do you mean?" Apple asked.

"I don't know. It just seems like after the posters went up for the Valentine Ball, everyone's mood changed. It's like you could feel it in the air. Some sort of nervous energy. Do you know what I mean?" Zen asked.

"I know what you mean. I can't believe how giddy people are acting. It's just a dance. I'm so not like that."

"You're not?" Zen said.

"No, I'm more of a low-expectation kind of gal," Apple admitted.

"Oh, you are, are you?" Zen asked, flashing her that dimpled smile. Was he flirting with her, Apple wondered?

"Yes. I think school dances are kind of silly," Apple continued.

"You do?"

"Well, yes. I mean, are school dances even fun? They seem to have a lot of pressure on them," she added cynically.

Whenever Apple had high expectations, things never turned out as she thought they would, kind of like New Year's Eve. She knew that whenever she didn't have expectations, she usually ended up having a better time. Not that she'd ever been to a school dance before, to know what to really expect.

Of course, on the inside, Apple knew this line was all a crock. She did have high expectations—she just didn't want to jinx it. So she was just playing down how excited she was, especially that she might at least get a dance with Zen.

"Yeah. They do," Zen said. "You're totally right."

"I mean, everyone is walking around wondering if someone is going to ask them to be their date for the dance," Apple continued. Hint, hint, Apple thought.

"Don't they have a theme every year too?" Zen asked. "I think I remember hearing that."

"Right! I totally forgot about that. The theme! I wonder what it'll be?" Apple said, truly excited. "It would be cool to have a theme that included the music. Like swing."

"I hate swing music," Zen said. "God, I hate it. And all those people throwing each other around."

"Really? I think it's kind of sexy," Apple said. She loved watching reality-TV dance shows and couldn't believe that anyone could hate swing dance.

"No, I love hip hop. That would be cool," Zen said.

"Really?" asked Apple. "I never pegged you as that type."

"There's no way you'll be seeing me swing dancing," Zen laughed. He seemed to be friendlier than he ever had to Apple. Maybe he really trusted her now, after their talk the other day. Maybe he was finally seeing the real Apple, she thought.

"So you've been thinking about the dance too, then, you hypocrite," Apple tried to joke.

"So've you. I know, for example, that you have plans with your friends for, um, what do you guys call it? Pampering?" Zen said, again flashing that dimpled smile.

Oh, God. Happy must have told Zen that they were planning to go to Gossip for facials. That was embarrassing.

"Well, why not? If you can't beat 'em, join 'em," Apple said.

"You know, Apple. Let's take some of these boxes outside. They're starting to pile up. We can leave them with the valet so they'll be there when we get picked up."

"Sure," Apple answered, grabbing a large brown box.

Wouldn't it be so amazing if Zen asked her to the Valentine Ball, even if the theme was hip hop? Apple was so completely wrapped up in a fantasy of dancing closely to Zen, that she didn't notice a pothole in the pavement in front of her.

Her arms flailed as she tripped and lost her balance. She felt the boxes fall to the ground and then felt herself tumble backward—right into Zen's arms. He was quick and strong and caught her before she reached the ground.

Apple let herself sink into his arms. It felt . . . right. She didn't want to move.

"Wow! Falling for me again," Zen said, laughing.

"Sorry," she said, standing up slowly. "I can't believe I just did that."

"Women are always falling for me," Zen joked. "Or at least I wish they were."

"I bet women fall for you all the time," Apple said, blushing. "I'm just joking! I mean . . ."

"Well, at least *you* just did," Zen said.

"Yeah, and you caught me too!" Apple answered, flirtatiously, or at least as flirtatiously as she could.

They stood staring at each other in a comfortable silence. What a magical moment, Apple thought. Was it fate? Here she had been thinking about Zen, and when she tripped, he caught her like she was a baseball and he was a glove. He did it so effortlessly, too, thought Apple. They would be perfect dance partners.

"Hey," he said, taking his hand and pushing her hair out of her face. Apple blushed again and felt herself tingling. It felt nice to have Zen stand so close to her and brush her hair away. It was like a scene out of a romantic movie.

"You know, Apple. You have such great hair," he said.

"I do?"

"Yeah. There's just so much of it," Zen said.

"I know," said Apple.

"So, are you okay?" Zen asked, looking concerned. "Do you want me to get you a bottle of water or something?"

God, was Zen cute when he was concerned! And he looked like he really did care about her well-being. He started to rub her shoulders.

"I don't think so," Apple answered, though she felt dizzy. She knew it had nothing to do with her fall.

"Are you sure? Should we take a break? Shall we go?" he asked.

"I think I'm okay," she answered. "I'm just a little woozy."

Zen cared! He cared! When he stopped massaging her shoulders, Apple felt a little upset. Still, they could stand like that forever.

They began picking the clothes up from the ground.

"Are you sure you're all right?" Zen asked again.

"I'm sure. Don't worry about me so much," Apple said.

"Good, because you're my number-one partner right now, and it would be a bummer if we couldn't volunteer together. I have fun with you."

"So, what were we talking about before I fell for you?" Apple tried to joke.

"The Valentine Ball," Zen said.

"Right. Well, like I said, it's so strange to see people so worried about what they're going to wear, and who they're going with," Apple continued, as they walked back into the club.

She knew that now was her chance. She could ask Zen to the dance, and let him think she was asking to go just as friends. Then, once he saw her looking fabulous, he'd really start to notice her. He had just looked like he really cared about her. He had even said he couldn't work without his number-one partner, and that he had fun with her. He had said he loved her hair!

"I'm thinking of asking Happy," Zen said, as they took their seats back behind the table.

Apple suddenly felt as if she might fall to the ground again, but this time because she really felt dizzy. Zen did not just say that he was thinking of asking Happy to the dance, did he?

Hadn't he just caught her? Wasn't that fate? Didn't they just share a magical moment? She had fit into his arms so perfectly. He had just told her he had fun with her, loved working with her, and now he was saying that he was going to ask Happy to the dance?

This cannot be happening, Apple thought.

"Really?" she asked, trying to not have a look of disenchantment on her face.

"Yeah," he said, as if it weren't such a big deal.

When Apple didn't respond, Zen spoke again. "Why? Do you think it's a bad idea?"

"No, it's not that," Apple began.

"Well, it must be something. I can read your face," Zen said. "Come on! Tell me. I trust what you have to say."

"You do?" Apple asked, thinking, why?

"Of course. Not only are you a good listener, but

also you're the Queen of Hearts's daughter. You must have picked something up by osmosis or whatever."

"Oh, you think so, do you? You haven't watched one of her shows, have you, ever?"

"No. Anyway, do you think Happy will turn me down?" he insisted.

"I don't know," Apple said. She felt sick.

"Well, you must know something. You're her best friend," Zen said.

"Honestly, I haven't talked to Happy today. But I do know what my mother would tell you to do—if you are at all interested in what the Queen of Hearts would have to say."

"But of course I am," Zen said. "How could I ever turn down free advice from the Queen of Hearts? I mean, I know she said not to be desperate. But a few days have gone by now, so I don't think I'd seem desperate."

"You're right. But my mother, the expert, would also say, play a little hard to get."

"Really? This is way too confusing for a guy," Zen moaned.

"She'd say that the modern woman should even go as far as to ask a guy to a dance—since it *is* the modern day and not the 1950s."

"I guess that makes sense," Zen said. "This starting a relationship thing is so tricky. No wonder I haven't had a girlfriend before."

"Well, millions of people a day think my mother makes perfect sense. Who could argue with the masses?" Apple said.

"Again you've given me something to think about.

Thanks Apple," he said.

As they finished up and said goodbye, Apple could tell by the focused look on his face that he was thinking about what she had told him.

She walked home fuming, and also feeling ashamed and embarrassed at her herself. How could she have mistaken his catching her for anything but his catching her? Why did she think it was fate? Luckily, Crazy Aunt Hazel was home. Aunt Hazel was always doing worse things than she had just done. Aunt Hazel would put things in perspective for her.

"Yo!" her aunt said when she walked in. She was standing in the kitchen, eating ice cream right out of the container.

"Yo!" Apple said back.

"So what's happening, do-gooder?"

"Nothing. What's happening here? Is Mom home?" Apple asked.

"Of course not. Duh!"

"Where's Dad?" Apple asked.

"He said he had some work to do and went to his office. Or maybe he went golfing. Who knows?"

"Oh," Apple said. She swore she could still feel Zen's arms wrapped around her. She could still feel the tingles on her face when he brushed her hair out of her eyes. "I thought it was date night," Apple asked her aunt. "Aren't Thursday nights date night?"

"Sweetie, when is the last time an actual date night took place?" Aunt Hazel asked her, giving her a look of self-pity.

Apple hadn't realized it, but Aunt Hazel was right. Her

parents hadn't been on one of their date nights in months.

Thursday nights had always been her parents' regular date night. Come hell or high water, they'd go out together, for dinner and a movie, after her mother's show. Apple remembered her father sometimes even buying flowers for her mother and knocking at the front door, pretending to pick up his wife for their date. When he used to do that, Apple wanted to be anywhere but near them. It was so embarrassing to watch her parents carry on like they were teenagers. But now Apple kind of missed the ritual, no matter how awkward it was to be around.

The next day after date night, her parents would act all sickeningly sweet to each other, and her mother would leave the house later than usual. That hadn't happened in a while, though. Apple couldn't even remember the last time it had happened.

"Your parents' marriage is falling apart, I think," said Aunt Hazel, putting the lid back on the ice cream container and throwing it back into the freezer.

"Why do you say that?" asked Apple, defensively and aggressively. It irked her that her aunt had also noticed what she had been noticing.

"Well, my assessment of the situation is that they just don't spend enough time together. Even when they're both at home, they don't hang out in the same room. It's like they're roommates. I'm telling you, something is going to have to change or pretty soon they're going to be sleeping not only in different rooms but in different houses."

"How would *you* know?" asked Apple, resentfully.

"Trust me. I've been in enough bad relationships to know when someone else's relationship is bad."

Apple had the thought that maybe everyone in her house was in some sort of relationship trouble. Maybe the troubles she was facing were the problems everyone faced at every age. And how could she expect to *not* be messed up about relationships when her house, as Brooklyn would say, was full of bad vibes? Not one person in this house, thought Apple, is not messed up.

fifteen

"You know, Hopper asked me to the Valentine's Day dance," Happy told Brooklyn and Apple as they walked into the doors of Gossip.

"He did what?" Apple and Brooklyn responded in unison.

"He did not!" Brooklyn added.

"He did," Happy said, as calmly if she were asking someone to pass the salt at dinner.

"That is amazing, Happy," Apple said. It *is* amazing, thought Apple—maybe my luck is changing. Apple totally hadn't been expecting this. Maybe Happy would go with Hopper as her date. Apple daydreamed that it was at least a possibility. Maybe Zen would be so bummed out to find out that someone had asked Happy before he did, that he'd be happy just to have a date at all.

"I've always thought he was kind of cute," Apple said to Happy. "Well, I mean, everyone knows he's cute."

"Yeah, he is really cute," answered Brooklyn dreamily.

"Well, I don't know what to do," moaned Happy, her blaséness wearing off. "I wish he hadn't asked me."

"Why, don't you like Hopper?" Apple said. "He's not always so bad. Brooklyn's right. He can be kind of funny, you know, if you like that kind of humor. And, as Brooklyn always says, things always happen for a reason. There must be a reason he asked you, Happy!"

"Yeah, he can be funny. And he can be nice," Happy responded. "I'm just . . . I'm just not sure. Maybe there is a reason."

"Maybe there is," Brooklyn said. "But Happy, be honest. You're waiting for a certain someone to ask you, aren't you?" she asked. "No judgment."

"Maybe," Happy answered.

Apple knew Happy was thinking about Zen. "Well, I don't know," she said to her friend. "If I were you, I'd accept the invitation. What did you tell him?" she asked. She was starting to worry. Only moments ago, she had been daydreaming of going with Zen, and that all her problems were solved.

"I told him I'd get back to him," Happy said. "He was very sweet when he asked. I've never heard him sound so compassionate before."

"And he was okay with that?" Brooklyn said.

"He seemed to be. Why, would you say yes?" Happy asked Brooklyn. "God, I don't know what to do. What would you do?"

"I guess I would say yes," Apple said. "Because, I don't know, it just seems more fair to accept the invitation that comes first. I mean, that's what I think. Plus, you said he was compassionate. Maybe it *is* fate. Maybe by you going with him, it will turn him into a nicer person. Yes, definitely, take the guy who asks you first."

"Why?" Brooklyn asked. "She's not the deli counter. It's not a first-come, first-serve basis. Not that I would ever eat meat," she added, "but you know what I mean."

"I know. That's not what I meant," Apple said. "I just meant that I wouldn't want to hurt Hopper's feelings. I mean, it's just a dance, and he must be sort of brave to have asked Happy. And so nicely."

"Maybe Apple's right," Brooklyn admitted. "It *is* just a dance. No need to lose any sleep over it. Find your inner peace. Follow your heart. Everything always works out."

"Well, I *have* been losing sleep," said Happy. "Can I tell you guys something, if you promise not to judge me? It's just that I was kind of hoping someone else would ask me."

"Like who?" asked Brooklyn, rolling her eyes at Apple.

"Zen. I wanted Zen to ask me."

"Duh! Like I said, you should always follow your heart," said Brooklyn. "Why don't you just ask him?"

Apple turned and looked at Brooklyn, stunned that her friend would suggest such a thing. How could Apple have known that Happy really, really had wanted to go with Zen, that she was losing sleep over it? And she was the one who had advised Zen to keep it cool!

"Maybe she wants to know that he wants to ask her," Apple said slowly.

"Well, you guys have given me a lot to think about," Happy said. "Now let's just enjoy our facials. I'm totally stressed about this. I need some pampering."

Two evenings later, Apple and Brooklyn were in Happy's big kitchen, making s'mores. Sailor had just stormed out of the house, after Happy refused to admit that she had borrowed her jeans, which Apple knew she had done.

"I think I'm going to take your advice," Happy said suddenly from the chair in the corner where she'd been sitting watching her friends cook.

"About what?" Apple asked.

"Going to the Valentine Ball dance with Hopper. I think I should just go with him," she said. Apple could tell Happy wasn't thrilled at the prospect. Her voice sounded beaten down, deflated like a two-day-old helium balloon. She looked tired, too, and washed out, sitting in a fetal position on a chair. And Happy always looked flushed and healthy.

"Why?" Apple asked, trying to sound supportive and concerned.

"I don't know. If Zen really wanted to ask me, I think he would have by now. I mean, the dance is just over a week away. Obviously, he doesn't really want to ask me or he would have. And, you're right— I don't want to be the one to ask him. I *do* want to know that he really wants to go with me," Happy said. "And Dr. Caffeine agrees. Plus, you're right— maybe it's fate."

"Maybe he just hasn't gotten around to it," Apple suggested.

"Maybe. But I talk to him every day at school, and we e-mail each other almost every night. There has been plenty of time to ask, and he just hasn't. It's just so frustrating. I don't know what's going on in his head," Happy said. "Sometimes I think he really likes me, but at other times, he just seems so distant. I don't get it."

"Well, if it makes you feel any better," Apple said, "I think you'll have a great time with Hopper. He's fun. And at least someone asked you."

"Someone really cute!" added Brooklyn eagerly.

"Yeah, you're right. Plus, it *is* just a stupid school dance, like you said. It's no big deal. Pass me the phone," Happy said, using her chin to point out where the phone was. Her hand was covered in chocolate sauce and Apple watched as she wiped it off on a towel. Apple handed her the phone.

"What? You're going to call him now?" she asked.

"Sure. Why not? What time better than the present?"

"Right," said Brooklyn, as they watched Happy dialing. "Live in the moment."

"Message coming," Happy said, after a brief pause.

"Hey, Hopper, it's Happy. I thought about it, and I'd love to accept your invitation to the dance. I'm looking forward to it. So, I guess I'll see you at school tomorrow. Cheerio!"

Apple couldn't believe how easy-breezy Happy sounded. How did she talk to the opposite sex so confidently, especially when her heart really wasn't in it? She *was* a good actor.

"Well, I guess that's done," Happy said. "No turning back now."

"Happy! Hopper is super hot, and we'll all be there. You'll have fun," Apple said, trying to cheer up her friend.

"Yeah, you're right. It will be fun," Happy answered, plastering a smile on her face.

"That's right, Happy," Brooklyn agreed. "If you smile on the outside, you'll begin to feel better about everything on the inside." She reached for her big toe and raised her leg straight up high into the air, while smiling, as if to prove her point.

When Apple got home, she couldn't stop thinking that Zen was now clear. He was dateless! Maybe this turn of events meant that she and Zen were fated to be together. It was all about timing, perhaps. Maybe everything *did* happen for a reason.

There was no way she could feel what she had felt when Zen's arms were around her if they weren't meant to be. There was no way. And if it had felt that good when she fell accidentally into his arms, how good would it feel to have his arms purposely wrapped around her?

She fell asleep with a smile on her face.

"Hey, Happy," Hopper said the next morning at the spiral staircase.

"Hey, Hopper," Happy said and smiled at him.

"I got your message last night," he said.

"Oh yeah? Good," Happy said, and smiled more sweetly.

"Yeah, so do you want me to pick you up at home, or do you want to meet here?" Hopper asked her.

"What are you guys talking about?" Zen threw in, looking at both of them.

"Happy accepted my invitation to take her to the Valentine Ball," Hopper said casually.

Apple immediately looked up at Zen. But he was retying his shoelaces, and not looking up. She couldn't catch his eye. The expression on his face was pained.

Oh, God, thought Apple. This is my fault. She felt horrible looking at Zen, who looked horrible. Even though Apple did not want him asking Happy to the dance, and wanted Happy to go with someone else, she didn't want Zen to find out this way.

Just then Poppy, the head of the clothing drive, walked by, calling out, "Thanks so much, Apple and Zen, for doing such a good job for the clothing drive! It's much appreciated! Just one more day!"

Zen simply nodded at Poppy, and Apple said to her, "No problem."

The bell rang and there was a rush to gather notebooks and knapsacks.

No one was quicker gathering their things than Zen, who had already jumped down the last two stairs and was heading toward class—except for Happy, who had hurried off leaving a trail of her signature peach scent.

"Zen?" Apple called out, catching up and grabbing his arm. She didn't know exactly what to say. But she knew she had to say something.

"What?" he growled. Apple was taken aback. He had never sounded unfriendly to her before.

"Are we meeting today to go over to the club after school?" Apple asked. It was the only thing she could think of to say at that moment.

"I guess we have to. It's the last time, right?" Zen said.

"Apparently," said Apple.

"I'll meet you by the front doors after school," Zen said, and walked off.

"Bye!" Apple called out after him.

But Zen didn't turn back or respond. Apple had a hard time catching her breath.

She couldn't pay attention to any of her classes all day. Everyone seemed to be in a foul mood, even the teachers. Mr. Kelly gave a pop quiz.

"Did you know?" Zen asked, as soon as Apple walked up to him at the front door after school. It seemed as if he had been waiting all day to ask her the question.

Happy had left early, for an "emergency" session with Dr. Caffeine, Brooklyn had told Apple, before she left for her yoga class.

"Did I know what?" Apple asked, even though she knew what he was getting at.

"Did you know that Happy was going to the dance with Hopper?" Zen asked resolutely.

Apple had two choices. The first was that she could lie and tell Zen that she had no idea, and that she had found out the same time he did, at the spiral staircase that morning.

But Apple felt exhausted. She didn't want to lie or tell half-truths anymore.

"I did know," she told him. "Well, I found out last night. I was at Happy's house and she called him and told him she'd go with him."

"So you knew that Hopper had asked her," he said.

"Well, I guess so. I mean, I found out just the other day. But I didn't know that she was going to accept until yesterday night. Didn't Hopper tell you?" Apple asked. "I mean, didn't he at least mention to you that he was thinking of asking Happy?"

"No," Zen said huffily. "Why would he?"

"I don't know. I thought you guys were good friends," Apple said.

"We are. But we don't talk about things like that. We're guys."

"Oh. Right," Apple said. She didn't know what else to say.

They walked in silence in the direction of the club. Zen walked quickly, so that Apple was always two steps behind him.

"Why didn't you say anything?" Zen said suddenly, stopping in his tracks.

"I don't know. I just didn't think it was important. And she's my best friend. I don't usually go around telling people what's going on in her life," Apple answered.

They continued to walk along in silence, Zen still walking ahead of Apple. But it was as if he couldn't contain himself. He stopped in his tracks again and looked Apple in the face.

"You told me that I should play it cool. That I shouldn't rush into asking someone to the dance. That's what you told me," he said loudly. He was one notch away from yelling, Apple could tell.

"No, I told you that's what *my mother's* advice would be!" Apple corrected him.

"Well, it didn't work!" he scoffed.

"I never said it would work! I mean, no one can see into the future. She's not a fortune teller. She just gives out advice!" Apple tried explaining.

"Well, it was bad advice. I should never have listened to it. I mean, if I had just asked Happy when I wanted to, she would have been going with *me*, not Hopper."

"Yes, there is something to be said for going on your gut instinct," Apple said.

"Yeah. I snoozed and now I lose. I don't even want to go to the dance anymore. I just want the whole thing to be over and done with," Zen muttered.

Apple felt awful. She needed to make it up to Zen. She needed, more than anything, for Zen to not be mad at her. He clearly blamed her for the turn of events. And rightly so, Apple thought.

"Zen, I have an idea," she told him, grabbing his arm so he would have to stand still.

"It's not more advice from your mother, is it?" he asked, bitterly.

"No," Apple said.

She couldn't believe she was about to do what she was going to do, but she really wanted to. "Well, it's just an idea," she said. "But maybe if you went to the dance anyway and looked good and acted very charming to Happy, she'd spend most of the night with *you*. I mean, it's just the Valentine Ball. She's going with Hopper just as friends. You heard them this morning."

"I don't know," Zen said as if he seemed to be considering it.

"Come on! Don't give up now. You know what I'll even do for you?" Apple pressed, trying to sound more confident than she felt.

"What?"

"I'll go as your date. You know, so you don't have to show up alone. I think you could win Happy back, no problem. She may even think you look chivalrous," Apple said, trying to get him into the spirit.

This was so not how I wanted this to work out, thought Apple. I wanted to go with Zen, but not like this. Not like this at all. This was not how it was supposed to go down.

But maybe once Zen saw her in another light, he would think of her differently. Stranger things have happened.

"So, will you go to the Valentine Ball as my date?" Apple pressed.

"Thanks Apple, but I think I'll pass," Zen said, without taking even a moment to think about it.

God, no one can find out about this, Apple thought. Oh, God, she thought, what if Happy finds out that I knew that Zen wanted to ask her but that I didn't tell her?

Apple realized, for the first time, that she needed help. She needed to *talk* to someone. She obviously couldn't go to Happy or Brooklyn. Aunt Hazel, maybe? But her aunt was so crazy, and besides, Crazy Aunt Hazel couldn't figure out her *own* life.

Sitting together collecting clothes for the next hour was painful. Apple had no idea how to pretend to ignore that Zen had turned her down so cruelly. Zen didn't speak much either. Apple knew his mind was on Happy and Hopper. She busied herself by folding clothes.

As she watched Zen walk off after the hour, she thought that volunteering to get closer to him hadn't worked at all. In fact, now he was just mad at her. Why couldn't he just like me, Apple thought—why did it have to be so difficult?

As she walked home, she remembered some of her mom's opinions about the importance of sharing your feelings and asking for advice. She knew she had to take action, because she couldn't keep leading her life this way. She was even sincerely questioning if *she*, not Happy, was the one who needed a shrink, based on her actions in recent weeks. When had she turned from Good Apple into Rotten Apple?

It pained Apple to even think about it, but there was one person she knew she could ask for help. And that person was so easy to find, at least for Apple—her mother, Dr. Bee Bee Berg.

When she arrived home and headed to her bedroom, Apple locked the door. Apple never locked her door, but this time she needed to. She sat down at her desk, fired up her computer, and created an anonymous e-mail account and a fake e-mail name.

Where should she start? She knew that her mother and Guy preferred to answer the shorter e-mails rather than the ten-page-long ones Dr. Bee Bee Berg sometimes received from distressed, and possibly disturbed, viewers. She also knew that her mom and Guy loved e-mails that included a bit of flattery.

Apple began to type.

Dear Queen of Hearts,
I need your help. Only you can help me. I've been an awful friend, and I didn't even get the guy. Let me make a long story short. I was in love with a guy for a very long time. I never told him, or anybody. Suddenly—out of nowhere, it seemed—he started to like my best friend. My best friend is gorgeous, and I could never compete. She liked him back. I couldn't handle it. I guess you could say I tried to sabotage their relationship—not purposely, but I let it happen. Actually, sometimes it WAS on purpose. I led him to believe that she wasn't interested in him. I led her to believe that he wasn't interested in her. After telling my best friend to accept an invitation to a dance from a different guy who she wasn't into, I then asked the guy she WAS into to the same dance. He turned me down. I deliberately gave my best friend advice that no one who wants a relationship to work should ever follow. Now everything is a mess. I'm worried that my best friend will find out what I did. I'm worried that the guy will find out what I did, and that we will never get the chance to see if we were at all meant to be. Now I just want out without anyone getting hurt. Please respond at your earliest convenience. But time is of the essence, for reasons I won't get into.
Sincerely,
Bigmistakegirl

P.S. Love your show.
Apple

Apple reread the e-mail. Then she gulped, hit the Send key, and closed down her computer. Okay, that was done. And then, like in a nightmare you suddenly wake up from, Apple could barely catch her breath. Wait— did she sign herself "Apple" on the anonymous e-mail she sent her mother? Oh, my God. She was an idiot! Apple restarted her computer, which seemed to take hours to reboot. She bit her nails. She already knew, in her heart, what she had done. She typed in the password to her new e-mail account, clicked on Sent, and scanned immediately to the bottom of the message. There it was. Right after signing "Bigmistakegirl," there was also her *real* name, standing out as bright as Christmas lights.

How could she have let this happen? Breathe, Apple, just breathe. What are the chances that her mother, or Guy, would ever actually read the e-mail she had sent? After all, they received hundreds of e-mails a week. The only reason they had probably opened Happy's so quickly was that she had written in the subject line that it was from Apple's friend. Breathe, Apple, just breathe. She felt like she was holding her breath, even though she knew she was actually inhaling and exhaling. Maybe there was another girl out there with the unfortunate name Apple. But what were the chances of that? God, if only her name had been Anne or Jane or something normal she wouldn't be so worried. Apple hated herself. She couldn't even send a fake e-mail correctly. She needed help in more ways than one.

sixteen

a pple walked around the house aimlessly. She opened and shut the fridge door a dozen times. She flipped through old magazines. She had no idea what to do with herself—she felt restless, and like jumping out of or peeling off her skin. It had been three days of what had seemed like nothing less than torture. Every time she saw her mother, Guy, Hazel, or her father at home, she looked for signs that they had found out what she had done. Just yesterday, her father had stared at her strangely, Apple thought. But all he said was, "You know I love you, kid, right?"

And when Crazy Aunt Hazel said, out of the blue one evening, "I know what you did, missus!" Apple had felt her stomach do a somersault. It turned out Crazy Aunt Hazel was only complaining that Apple had finished the carton of her aunt's favorite ice cream.

Though Apple was paranoid, and was watching her family like a hawk, everyone in her house seemed to be acting totally normally, at least as normally as usual. She knew she should get outside and go for a walk—anything to get her away from her computer. She could walk down to Market Mall and look at clothes, but she had never felt so unattractive in her life, and she couldn't imagine even having the energy to try anything on. No, not even shopping would make her feel better right now. There was only one thing Apple wanted to do.

It was as if another person had taken over her body as she walked zombie-like upstairs to her mother's office.

She logged on, slowly typing out the letters P-A-S-S-W-O-R-D.

She scrolled down. The inbox seemed bottomless. Every day, it seemed, there were more and more e-mails from the lovelorn. No wonder her mother and Guy were always so busy. Heartbreak never took a vacation.

Apple scanned the From column, her heart pounding, and saw that the e-mail from her—from Bigmistakegirl—had been opened. I knew it, thought Apple. I just knew it—my mother read it already and maybe she even started to respond.

Apple was freaking out. Guy and her mother must know that *she* was Bigmistakegirl. They weren't stupid.

She clicked on Draft and saw two paragraphs that someone—her mother, or Guy—had written in response. Her eyes scanned quickly over the words, trying to make sense of them. But Apple couldn't focus. She had to think. She inhaled deeply.

Suddenly she heard heels clicking across the floor downstairs. Shit, thought Apple. My mother is home!

"Apple!" she heard her name being called. "Apple? Are you home? You left your jacket lying on the floor in the hallway, and all the lights are on down here."

There couldn't possibly be a worse time for her mother to show up. She hadn't finished reading the response to her e-mail! She needed to know what her mother's advice was.

What should I do? thought Apple frantically, jumping up from the chair, looking desperately at the screen. What should I do? She couldn't read while hearing her mother's heels clicking closer and closer.

She heard her say, "Apple? Are you here?"

I know! I'll just forward my mother's response to my account, thought Apple. That way I can read it later from the privacy of my own room. "Apple?" her mother called out again. "What are you doing up here?"

"Um, yeah!" Apple called back. "I'm up here!"

Her mother climbed the stairs and entered the office.

That was too close, thought Apple. She didn't turn around to face her mother.

"I was just, um, using your computer because mine has a virus and kept shutting down," Apple stuttered at the screen. Her face felt like fire. She felt faint.

"Well, hurry up then. I need to get on it. Do you think you need another computer? We can go out this weekend and buy one for you," her mother said, sitting down on a nearby chair and kicking off her shoes. She began massaging her feet.

"Thanks, that's okay. I'm sure it will work out. I'll just be a minute," Apple said.

She clicked on to the Sent page to make sure she had forwarded the e-mail to her account. But something seemed wrong. Apple looked more closely at her mother's response, which she thought she had forwarded. Why in the To line did it show Happy's name and e-mail address? Oh. No. No. No. No. No. NO!

"Oh my God," screamed Apple.

"What? What is it?" her mother asked, jumping off her chair and racing over. "What happened? What's wrong?"

Her mother looked over Apple's shoulder at the screen.

"What are you doing reading the letters to the Queen of Hearts?" she asked, flabbergasted.

"I was just . . . I was just . . ." Apple couldn't form a complete sentence. Her mind was on what else she had just done. How had she accidentally forwarded her letter and her mother's response to Happy? She knew it had been because she was so flustered to hear her mother come in, along with the fact that she had been thinking about Happy. She must have typed in Happy's name instead of her own.

Then her mother started yelling at her, like she had never heard her mother scream before.

"Apple! Are you reading my mail? Apple, I asked you a question," Dr. Berg demanded. "That looks like one of my responses! Answer me right now, young lady! I've told you before that you have to respect readers' privacy."

Apple couldn't take the pressure anymore. She couldn't take one more thing going wrong in her life.

"Yes, Mother! I was. You caught me. I was looking at your private e-mails, and I've been doing it for weeks," she screamed, getting out of the chair and slamming her hand on the table. It actually felt good to let it out. At least for a split second it did.

"You *know* you're not supposed to do that! And just how did you get in, anyway?" her mother yelled.

"Because your password is *password*! Everyone in this house knows that!" Apple yelled back.

"Wait. *You're* the Apple who sent me that question! My God, I thought there was another Apple out there. I was even going to tell you about it. It was *you*? YOU?" her mother gasped, slapping her hand on her forehead. "It was YOU! I cannot believe this," her mother said, sounding bowled over.

"Yes, fine! It was me! Me!" Apple said, holding up her hands as if to say, "I've been caught!"

Dr. Berg grabbed her daughter by both shoulders. "Apple, you're grounded!" It was the first time Apple's mother had ever used that sentence. "You are *grounded*. I'm mortified, just mortified by what you have done to your friend. And, as a professional, I'm also mortified that you would take advantage this way. Not to mention that I'm also mortified, as your mother, that I raised a daughter who would think any of this was okay."

"I don't care! My life is over anyway," Apple screamed, escaping from her mother's hands.

Oh, God, Happy would see not only her mother's response, but also every word Apple had written *to* her mother—everything she had done. And her stupid, stupid name. Yes, Apple's life was definitely over. O-V-E-R.

She stormed away from her mother, who was now sitting on a chair, resting her hands on her head and her elbows on her knees, as if she was suffering from a very bad migraine. Apple took the stairs down two by two to her bedroom, and slammed the door.

She searched frantically for her phone. She had no idea if her mother was about to come down and take away all her electronic gadgets. She wasn't sure exactly what her mother meant by her being grounded, since it had never happened before. She couldn't find the phone anywhere. God, she really was turning into her crazy, totally disorganized aunt Hazel, who lost her home phone—in her home—for days sometimes. Apple finally found her cell phone in her bag.

She pressed down hard on the number 1 key, the speed dial to Happy.

For as long as Apple could remember, Happy had been number 1 on her speed dial. Pick up, Happy, pick up, Apple willed in her head.

"Hello, Apple," she heard Happy say, after it rang twice. Apple could tell, by Happy's tone, that all was not cool. Apple took a deep breath.

"Hi, Happy. Listen. There's something I need to talk to you about," Apple said. She felt faint, and her heart was pounding a million beats per second. It was the exact same feeling she used to have when old Zen passed her in the hallways. But this was worse—way worse. She felt desperate. What was it her mother always said? Something about the truth being the best way to get out of sticky situations?

"And what would that be?" Happy asked in a snarky tone. Of course, Apple's last hope of explaining *before* Happy saw the e-mail had collapsed. Happy had been carrying around her BlackBerry like it was glued to her ever since she and Zen had started e-mailing each other. All Happy's e-mails were forwarded to her BlackBerry. She had probably got the e-mail one second after Apple had sent it by mistake.

"Okay," Apple said, swallowing. "Well, an e-mail was sent to you that was not supposed to be sent to you."

"Really?" Happy said the way she would to a three-year-old. "Do explain."

Apple suddenly felt exhausted, as if she hadn't slept in months. She was tired of playing games. She was tired of lying. With one hand, she wiped away tears that had formed like big raindrops. "I know you read it," she said. "I can tell by the sound of your voice."

"You're right, Apple. I did read it," Happy answered.

Apple felt miserable. She needed to make things right again with her best friend, at any cost. Though Apple dreaded confrontation, she knew she couldn't avoid it now.

"Can I explain, please?" Apple pleaded. "Please, just let me explain."

"You can try," Happy said, sounding bored. Apple could imagine her sitting there filing her nails.

But she felt a surge of hope. If Happy would at least let her explain what had happened, then maybe she would understand and forgive her. Maybe she'd understand that, like Dr. Bee Bee Berg always said in her show, one should never underestimate what heartbreak can do to a woman. And Apple was going to tell the truth, finally. That should count for something.

"Well," she began, "I had feelings for Zen. Actually, I've had a huge crush on him for, like, two years. I never told you. I never told anyone. It's like you guys always call me—I'm the Sponge. And I didn't want to jinx it. Crazy Aunt Hazel always talks so optimistically about her men the second she meets one, and it always ends in disaster. I didn't want that to happen. And I didn't want you to think that I was pathetic for liking him for so long and not telling you about it. And what if he never liked me? I don't want to end up like Aunt Hazel, hurt all the time. But then you started liking him, and I was torn. I know what I did was awful. I know I should have told you right at the beginning. I know I shouldn't have tried to sabotage your relationship. I didn't want to—I just couldn't help it. One thing led to another and it got completely out of hand. I never meant to hurt you, Happy. I would never do that. You're my best friend. You know that," Apple said, choking out her last words with tears.

There was a pause.

"If you liked Zen so much, why would you want to hurt him?" Happy asked. "That's what I really would like to know."

"I didn't want to hurt Zen. I didn't want to hurt him at all," Apple professed.

"Well, you did," Happy said.

"No, I didn't. I know he still likes you. That hasn't changed. That never changed."

"I know he does," Happy said. "Trust me, I *know* he still likes me."

"See?" Apple said, getting excited. Maybe it would all work out. Maybe Happy wasn't that mad, after all. Now that she knew that Zen still liked her, maybe everything would be fine. Maybe Happy wasn't that pissed off. She still had the man—this was just a little bump in the road of their friendship. All friendships had bumps in the road, didn't they?

"He's pissed too," Happy said.

"Oh, I know he's pissed because he's not going to the Valentine Ball with you. But I'm sure he'll still show up and you and him can still spend the dance together. I'm sure Hopper won't mind. He'll understand," Apple said, her mouth becoming drier and drier.

"No, he's not pissed at that. Well, he *is* pissed at that, but he's also pissed at what you did," Happy said.

Apple was puzzled. "But he doesn't have to find out," she said, desperately trying to convince Happy. "Honestly, this is just a huge misunderstanding. None of this should have ever have happened. Zen still likes you. You still like Zen. Isn't that the important thing? Isn't that all that matters at the end of the day?"

"He's already found out," Happy said. "I called him and told him about the e-mail you, ahem, *accidentally* sent to me. In fact, I forwarded it to him just two seconds before you called."

The room was spinning. Apple felt like she was locked in an elevator that was falling down fast. Not only did Happy know everything she had done, but Zen did too. Zen. Zen. Zen.

"Anyway," Happy continued, snob-like—a tone Apple had rarely, if ever, heard from Happy. "He also told me that you asked him to the Valentine Ball. That's nice, Apple. Really nice—and after you told me that I should go with Hopper. You just wanted me to go with Hopper so you could swoop in and ask Zen."

"No! That's not right at all! I only asked him so he would go to the dance because he was so upset that you were going with Hopper," Apple tried to explain. "I thought once I got him there, he'd be cheered up just to see you!"

"Seriously, Apple. How can I trust anything you say now?" Happy asked.

"You can, Happy. You can," Apple cried. "This was the first time I've ever lied to you. Ever!"

"Oh, and Apple? How would your mother feel if she found out what you did?"

"Well, actually, she did find out," Apple groaned. "I'm grounded."

"Hah! She wasn't pleased to find out her daughter was going around pretending to be her, breaking up relationships, and screwing her so-called best friend? I wonder why not?"

Apple had no idea how to respond. How could she explain to her best friend that she, Apple, was still trust-worthy? Before she could answer, Happy started to speak again.

"Is there anything else you'd like to get off your chest while you have the chance? Any more deep secrets? Is your name even Apple?"

Apple swallowed and tried to ignore her friend's sarcastic tone. "Just that I'm sorry. I'm so, so sorry," Apple said. "I hope you can find it in your heart to forgive me. It will never happen again. I promise."

"You know what, Apple?" Happy asked.

"What?" Apple said.

"I know it won't happen again. I believe you when you say that," Happy said.

"You do?" Apple asked quietly, with hope.

"Yes, I do. But I can't forgive you. We can't be friends anymore. I could never forget what you've done to me," said Happy. "This friendship is so over. It's so very over."

Apple heard the click at the other end of the line.

She realized, minutes later, that she was still holding the phone.

How was it possible, with one click of the phone, that their whole history—years of friendship—was over? That was it? A decade of talking almost every day, done just like that?

Apple wasn't ready to let that go. Not without a fight. She called Happy back, but got her voice mail.

Apple didn't leave a message. Not the first time she got Happy's voice mail, and not the ninth time. She had no idea what to say anyway, even if she could get through to Happy herself. She sat down on her bed, her phone still glued to her hand.

There was a knock at her bedroom door.

"Apple, it's me. I'm coming in," she heard her mother say.

Great, thought Apple.

"I've decided we need to talk about this." Dr. Bee Bee Berg sat down on Apple's desk chair and crossed her legs. "I just reread what you sent to me. I just don't get it, Apple," her mother said. She got up and sat on the bed next to her daughter.

"What don't you get?" Apple asked her mother, looking at the floor. Did anyone still love her? she wondered. "I mean, you're the expert, aren't you? You're the expert about all things love and relationships."

"First off," her mother said, "I don't understand why you would do that to your friend. I don't understand why you would try to ruin your friend's relationship. And I really don't understand why you would sneak into my private e-mails."

"You don't get it? *You* don't get it?" Apple said, sitting up to attention and turning to look her mother in the eye. "You, of all people, do *not* get why I would sneak into your private e-mail."

"No, I don't 'get' it. Apple, you of all people should know that trying to ruin a blossoming relationship leads to no good. If two people are meant to be together, they will end up together. How could you not know this? You are around when Guy and I speak. You've grown up with my advice around you. You should know, more than anyone else, that all is *not* fair in love and war, and that sometimes you just have to accept that."

Apple grabbed her hair as if she were going to rip it out. "You think you are so good at fixing other people's problems, but you can't even fix your own. You're always willing to shell out relationship advice to other people, but you can't follow it yourself. Why should I listen to you when your own relationship sucks?"

Apple laughed. "I may not have a relationship, but at least I'm not in a bad one."

"Apple!" her mother exclaimed, standing up. Apple had never seen Dr. Bee Bee Berg look so shocked, not even the time a guest on her show admitted to cheating on her husband for twenty years straight.

"Well, it's true, Mom. You want to get into it and have a serious discussion? Fine. Let's do it. Why is Dad sleeping in the spare bedroom? Why has he been sleeping there for weeks? Did you really think I hadn't noticed? If your own marriage is so perfect, then why don't you spend any time with Dad? Are you that willing to give him up for the sake of your career? Why do youspend ninety-nine percent of your time with Guy?" Apple was crying now, but she couldn't stop. "How can you not see how upset you make Dad? How can you not see that he's going to leave you if you don't spend some time with him? How can you not see that he hates coming home? That he hates coming home to an empty house? How can you not see what is happening right here in your own home?"

Dr. Bee Bee Berg didn't say anything. She just sat back down, blinking her eyes rapidly and pursing her lips.

But Apple wasn't done.

"And you talk so much about the importance of people's privacy, but you are such a hypocrite," she continued.

"What are you talking about now?" her mother asked almost inaudibly.

"I'm talking about *you* sneaking into *my* computer and reading my PRIVATE diary entries. Who gave you the right to come into my room and read my diary? It's so pathetic."

"Apple, I have no idea what you are talking about. I don't even know how to turn your computer on. And I would never—*never*—read your private diary entries. I never even knew you kept a diary," her mother said defensively.

"That's bull, Mom, and you know it. What about your lecture to me about how I'm young and I should have a boyfriend my own age? You went on about that for days. And it's because you read my diary entry about me being in love with Mr. Kelly. You started lecturing me immediately after I wrote that. And guess what, Mother? It was a fake entry I wrote just to trap you. And it worked. You read it, and you started in on me about it. So you knew. Don't lie to me," Apple screamed. "You knew!"

"Apple, it is true that I knew," her mother said. "But I didn't go into your room. I didn't sneak into your diary entries. Hazel told me about the crush."

Apple knew, by the way her mother was speaking so warily, that she wasn't lying. Suddenly Apple had a very bad headache. She lay back on her bed.

She never thought the day would come when she would actually want her mother to ask, "How are you feeling? Do you want my advice?" But that's exactly what she wanted now, more than anything else in the world. She really, truly needed someone's advice.

seventeen

as if nothing had happened, Crazy Aunt Hazel was honking at 8 a.m. sharp to take Apple to school.

Not going to school was not an option—Apple's mother had made that very clear. Now that Apple was grounded, it was the *only* option. After school, she was to come straight home. There would be no going out, not even for a walk.

"Hi, Apple," her aunt said breezily when Apple opened the passenger door.

"Don't 'hi' me," Apple huffed, pulling the seatbelt strap over her body.

"What's *your* problem?" Aunt Hazel asked her, checking the rearview mirror and pulling out of the driveway.

"You of all people know perfectly well what my problem is," Apple retorted.

"I know you're grounded, but that's your own doing. Don't take it out on *me*," Aunt Hazel said like a child.

"I may be crazy, but I'm not crazy enough to do what *you* did!" She laughed. "Sure, I've had my moments, but I'd never pretend to be your *mother* giving out advice!"

"Ha, ha. I'm so glad you think it's so funny that my life is ruined. And I only went into her private documents because I thought she was going through mine, thanks to you," Apple said, looking out the window.

"Oh, God, Apple. You should know your mother better than that. She would never go through people's things. She respects people's privacy," Aunt Hazel said. "She was furious with me for reading your diary. She was livid! But you should know that she'd never do that to you."

"Yeah, thanks. I know that now. But obviously *you* don't! How could you do that to me? How could you go into my private diary?" Apple demanded, turning back to face her aunt.

"Apple, I was concerned," her aunt told her.

"Right. Whatever," Apple said sullenly.

"I was! I didn't mean to pry. But I wanted to update my online dating profile. I think expressing an interest in aerobic striptease was getting me the wrong kind of interest back. I saw a folder called 'ED,' on your desktop and I was curious. I didn't know what ED was. I thought ED was a guy. And you never talk about anything. I just wanted to know what was going on in your life. And then I saw my name on the screen, and when you see your own name, you can't *not* read what's written about you. And, by the way," she added, "thanks for writing all those *very* nice things about me. I can't believe you think I'm so pathetic. I can't believe you think I throw tantrums! And that I'm a—what was it you wrote?—a reminder of how you don't want your life to turn out?"

"Well, I was just in a bad mood!" Apple said. "I didn't really mean it. But you *do* sometimes act very immaturely."

"Hey, I'm not the one who screwed things up with my best friend," Aunt Hazel snapped. "And all for a guy."

As soon as Hazel brought up Zen, Apple started to cry.

"Oh, honey. Don't cry. It will all work out," her aunt said, taking one hand off the wheel to hold Apple's hand.

"How do you know? How do you know it will all work out?" Apple asked desperately, between sobs.

Her aunt pulled gently on a curl and spoke softly. "Hey, I may be crazy, but I believe that things always happen for a reason. Maybe you had to go through all this to realize that Zen isn't the right one for you. And maybe this test will make your friendship with Happy stronger—in the long run. It might bring you closer."

"You really think so?" Apple asked through her tears, with a glimmer of hope.

"Oh, honey, what do I know? I'm just a walking, breathing memo reminding you how you *don't* want your life to end up, or so I've read." Hazel sighed.

"But what am I going to do? What am I going to *do*? Happy is so mad at me. Zen is so mad at me. My mother is so mad at me. I've ruined everything," Apple cried.

"You are going to walk into that school, holding your head up high," her aunt said, pointing up the street to Cactus High.

Apple couldn't look. "How can I? Everyone probably knows what I've done. Everyone probably hates me now. Happy does. And Zen does. And, who knows, Brooklyn probably is mad at me too, because I did something so bad for my soul or something."

"This is something you learn with age," Crazy Aunt Hazel said as she pulled up in front of the school. "And I want you to listen to this, even if you don't listen to me about anything else ever again. *No one* cares about *you* as much as you think they do. Trust me, they all have their own problems. They're not going to be focusing on yours. I bet ninety percent of the students in your school like someone who doesn't like them back. They're too wrapped up in their own problems to concentrate on what you did. Even though what you did *was* fairly rotten, most people screw up and make mistakes and hurt the people they love the most at some time. The most important thing is not to give up on relationships or friendships, even if it means getting snubbed or being embarrassed sometimes."

Apple looked gratefully at her aunt before taking a deep breath and getting out of the car. Aunt Hazel was mostly flaky, but sometimes she was also rather wise.

Feeling nervous, Apple walked through the school doors. She stopped just inside and looked over at the spiral staircase. Zen and Happy were there, along with Brooklyn and a couple of other students.

Apple knew there was no way she could walk up to them. What if she did and they saw her and turned away? She couldn't even think about that. She was not brave enough—not yet. So she turned and walked quickly in the opposite direction, to the washroom. She busied herself, pretending to fix her makeup and hair, for the ten minutes until the first bell rang, waited until the halls cleared, just to make sure she would not run into Zen or Happy or anyone else who might know what she had done, then raced to math class.

She stopped outside the door, took another deep breath, and walked into Mr. Kelly's class to her seat next to Happy. Happy did not look over at her once, for the entire hour, not even a sideways glance. When Happy put her mind to do something, she did it. When she said their friendship was over, Apple cried inwardly, she must have really meant it.

It was the most painfully long day at school.

Apple walked home after school feeling miserable. Not even the beautiful scenery could cheer her up today. Once at home, she fixed herself a sandwich— Cheerios on peanut butter, something that usually cheered her up, at least a little.

"Hellooo? Hellooo?" Guy sing-songed, sashaying into the kitchen.

"Oh, hey," Apple said, wiping her mouth.

"Hey to you," Guy said back, then stopped and looked her up and down. "What is up with you, girl? You look like crap."

"Thanks," Apple said. She knew she looked bad. But it was nothing compared to how she felt inside.

"Guy's sorry, but you do. You look all pale, and you have Louis Vuitton large bags under your eyes. Are you coming down with something?" he asked.

"Because if you are, stay away from Guy! Guy so *cannot* get sick right now. What's making you ill, little one?"

"Just life," Apple said, hiding her face behind her hair.

"Ah, *that* disease," Guy mocked. He paused. "Have you talked to your mother?"

"No, why?" Apple asked.

"Just that I haven't spoken to her since early this morning," Guy said, actually sounding concerned.

"That's weird. Haven't you seen her today? I mean, don't you guys talk like 128 times a day?" Apple said, putting her plate in the dishwasher.

"Usually we do, yes. Didn't you hear the big news?" Guy asked.

"Hear what big news?" Apple said, looking up at Guy. "*What* news?"

"That your mother has taken off like a bird," Guy said, fluttering his arms.

"What do you mean?" Apple asked, alarmed.

"She went on a romantic two-day getaway to Las Vegas."

"Oh my God! She ran away?" Apple asked, jumping up from her chair.

"She ran away with your *father*. She came to the office this morning and said, 'I think I'm going to go away with my husband.' Isn't that *romantic*? And then she kissed me on the cheek and walked out the door."

"They did *what*?" Apple exclaimed. "But what about the show?"

"Don't worry, we have those follow-up shows in the bank ready to go in case of emergency," Guy said.

"I can't believe it! Are you positive?" Apple asked again. "She just took off?"

"I know! Guy was a little worried. Actually, Guy was *very* worried. Your mother *hates* not being in the studio. But she was *very* adamant about it. She said, 'Just air the follow-up shows. I'm going *away* with my husband.' And I haven't heard from her since!"

"But I'm grounded!" Apple said. "How can she ground me and then take off to Vegas?"

"Oh, Apple. What have you done?" Guy said.

"Nothing. I don't want to talk about it. I mean, let's check the machine. Maybe Mom left a phone message."

Apple raced to the phone and dialed in the pass code.

"*You have three new messages,*" the automated voice said. "*First message.*"

Apple heard her mother's voice. "Hey, honey. It's Mom. Your dad and I are leaving town for a couple of days. I think this is just what we need. Hazel will be coming over and staying with you. Remember, you're still grounded, so no funny business—school, home, school, home. We're trusting you to be responsible about this." Her mother left the hotel room and number, ending the message with "If you need anything, just call. And Apple? I love you."

Apple gulped.

The second message was from her father. "Hey, kiddo. It's your dad. Just calling to let you know that your mom and I are taking a last-minute flight to Vegas. So don't worry if you don't hear from me. I'll put $100 on red for you. Speak to you soon, honey. I love you."

The third message was from her aunt. "Yo! This walking reminder of how you don't want your life to end up will be coming over to stay with you tonight and tomorrow night while your parents go do naughty things in Vegas. I'll be by around nine, after my date. Wish me luck! Actually, pray for me. But I'm supposed to be watching you, so if your mother calls, just say I'm in the washroom and I'll call her back."

Apple put down the phone. It *was* true. Her parents had gone away together for a romantic getaway. And Crazy Aunt Hazel's strike against men was officially over. She was going on a date after all.

"So?" Guy said. "Was there a message from her?"

"You're right," Apple said, shaking her head in disbelief. "They went to Las Vegas. Las Vegas! I can't believe it! It's so unlike them!"

"Guy knows. Guy doesn't know *what* got into your mother. But suddenly she became *very* passionate about your dad. Did she mention anything about the show?"

"No. She didn't. That's so weird too." She looked at Guy. "I mean, usually all she can talk about is the show. She didn't even ask me if I needed her advice about anything. She didn't even ask how I was *feeling*. Should I be worried?" Apple asked, troubled.

"We should *all* be worried. Guy can't believe she didn't say *anything* about the show! And it's going to be a good one on Monday. You'll never guess who's going to be a guest!"

"I'm sure I won't," Apple said.

"You want a hint? You know one of the guests who's coming on!" Guy said.

"I do?"

"Yes! But I just got off the phone with her moments ago, which is why she probably hasn't told you yet," Guy said.

"You can't believe *who* didn't tell me *what*?" Apple asked.

"Happy!"

"What are you talking about?" Apple said, alarmed.

"Happy is going to be a guest on *Queen of Hearts with Dr. Bee Bee Berg*! She is just too excited. It's so cute. Guy adores getting young people on the show. It brings a whole new, *je ne sais quoi* life to the show. You know what Guy means?" He clapped his hands gleefully.

"I do *not* know what you mean. What are you talking about? Why is Happy going on my mother's show? How can this be happening?" Apple groaned, a scowl forming on her face as she sank into a chair.

"Oh, don't be upset, Apple, that she didn't tell you. I'm sure she's going to. It all was just finalized like twenty minutes ago. That's why Guy was so excited to tell your mother. Guy just had to race over to see if she left me any last-minute notes in the office. Happy is probably just overwhelmed right now thinking about what she's going to wear!" Guy said.

"I can't believe this," Apple moaned.

"What? You're not jealous, are you?"

"Oh, God, no! I just don't want to talk about it."

"Do you want Guy to give you a hug? Would that make you feel better?" he asked, pulling her into a hug before she could answer.

Apple was grateful to her mother for not telling Guy anything about her falling out with Happy. She didn't want to explain to anyone else what she had done, or why she had done it. She untangled herself from Guy's embrace. It hadn't helped.

"So . . . what is the show's topic?" Apple asked fretfully. "What exactly is Happy going to talk about?"

"It's about relationship sabotaging. Well, relationship sabotaging part five or ten. We've done a lot of that show. Guy's lost count of how many. We do the show *every season*. People just love it. You know, *everyone* can relate to it."

"Why would Happy go *on television* in front of a million viewers to talk about that?" Apple asked.

"Sweetie, it's more like *10 million* viewers. It was all last-minute. Guy was booking guests, because, thanks to your mother suddenly taking off, all was left on Guy's shoulders. And Guy's *rude* guest for Monday bailed on him last minute. I should have figured as much. The show *was* going to be about men who have gone AWOL on their relationships. This guy, our main guy, was dating someone for two years and then suddenly just stopped calling and returning calls. He just disappeared from the relationship. Poof! Gone! Remind Guy *never* to rely on men who go AWOL on their relationships *ever* again," Guy said.

"Guy! Focus, please! Happy!" Apple said, jumping up and grabbing Guy by his slippery silk-shirted shoulders.

"Right. So anyway, just as Guy was freaking out with a capital F, wondering how he was going to get a last-minute guest to fill up Monday's spot, an e-mail—a very

196

nice and literate e-mail, Guy might add—arrived in his inbox, from Happy. You know, she's quite articulate. She's got beauty and brains, that one. You're lucky to have such a good friend like that."

I *was,* Apple thought, despondently.

"And then what happened?" Apple pushed.

"Well, Happy suggested that *The Queen of Hearts* has such a huge following among teenagers that we should do a show specifically *on* teenagers. Don't you think that's *such* a good idea? It's *brilliant.* And she offered herself up as a guest. Guy booked her, without even asking her what she could talk about, because she was so convincing. Also, Guy *was* in a bit of a panic to come up with a show. But then it came out that she just had this awful thing happen to her. A friend of hers tried to wreck her romance, and just before the Valentine Ball! Can you believe it? Anyway, Apple, isn't that fantastic? I mean, not for Happy, but for the show. Do you know that girl she's talking about?"

"Um, no," Apple said. She couldn't tell Guy. "I mean, I'm sure she'll tell me when we talk," she lied.

Apple was mortified. How could Happy do this to her? Oh, right. Why *wouldn't* Happy do this to her?

"Don't you have to run these things by my mother?" Apple asked. "I mean, doesn't she need to know who the guests are going to be?"

Guy laughed. "Of course not! She trusts Guy to book the guests. She trusts Guy with *everything.*"

"I think you should call her and tell her," Apple said. Maybe if her mother heard that Happy was going on her show to talk about relationship sabotaging, she would put her foot down and try to save Apple, her only child, from national mortification.

"Are you kidding me?" exclaimed Guy. "And *disturb* her romantic getaway with your father? No way. You know, Apple, Guy shouldn't be telling you this, but Guy really thinks this getaway is just the thing they need to get their marriage back on track. You might think that they have the *perfect* relationship, but even your mother and father need to make an effort sometimes. Even the Queen of Hearts could use some relationship therapy. You should have *seen* your father when he came to pick her up to go to the airport. He looked twenty years younger! So, no, Guy will *not* be disturbing them over this. And neither will *you*," he added pointedly.

It was true—this was her parents' first getaway in years. And Apple just couldn't break her father's heart by getting her mother to talk about work on their weekend away together. Especially not after Dr. Bee Bee Berg had actually listened to Apple's thoughts on her marriage and was now trying to put effort into it.

"So are you going to find out from Happy exactly what she plans to say on the show?" Apple asked Guy. "I mean, don't you pre-interview your guests?"

"Sometimes," Guy answered. "But usually it's better to not rehearse what they're planning to say. It ruins the spontaneity. We'll just get Happy to tell her story. You know, this could be Happy's big break! Didn't you say she always wanted to be an actress?"

"Yes," gulped Apple. "She does."

"Well, if she looks good on air, and speaks well, who knows what will come out of this for her! Don't tell anyone Guy said this, but viewers rarely remember what you *say*—they only remember if you looked good or not. *You'll* have some idea of what Happy is going to talk about. You're her best friend!" Guy said. "But what Guy *did* find out from her did sound pretty juicy!"

"Yes, I think I may have some idea," said Apple almost to herself. She looked at Guy again. "Did my mother say when she was coming back?"

"She said she would come straight from the airport to the studio on Monday for the show," Guy answered. He looked her up and down again. "God, girl. You should go take a hot bath with some essential oils and scented candles to relax you. You really do look like crap." Then, with a "ta ta," he sauntered out the door.

eighteen

$a$pple's eyes stung Monday morning. She wasn't sure if it was because of all the crying or from the lack of sleep—both of which had lasted the entire weekend. She felt like a convict. She hadn't left the house at all. Nobody had called, and no matter how many times she checked for a dial tone, her phone was still perfectly functional. The lives of everyone around her seemed to be fine and dandy. Crazy Aunt Hazel was seeing someone—at least she had made it to date three, which was pretty good for Aunt Hazel. Her parents were having the time of their lives in Vegas. From the sound of giddiness in her mother's voice on her voice-mail messages, it sounded like she was the teenager and Apple was the sober mother, worrying over what those two were up to.

She decided she couldn't possibly go to school today, which wasn't a problem for Crazy Aunt Hazel, who completely understood heartbreak. Her aunt was all about taking mental health days.

"Sometimes a gal just needs to take a mental health day," she had said, happily, as she prepared to go to work. "But I can't tell you how good I feel right now. Life is just so much better when you have someone to share it with—when you know someone is on your side, no matter what," she said.

"Please, Aunt Hazel, not now," begged Apple. "You've only been on three dates with this guy."

"Sorry, hon. I just haven't been this happy in a long, long time. This is it. He's the one! I'm so sure of it this time," she rhapsodized.

"And I'm happy for you. I am," said Apple, trying to sound more convinced than she felt. Not only was she a ball of misery, but she hated seeing her aunt get so excited about men when they usually turned out to be nothing but a bust.

After Hazel left, Apple headed back to her bedroom, planning on sleeping all day. But she couldn't. In nine hours, once Happy went on *The Queen of Hearts* and shared her story, Apple would officially be finished. She would be the laughing stock of the entire school. And the laughing stock of the entire country. Maybe the world— who knew where else *The Queen of Hearts* aired? She slipped out of bed and headed downstairs in her pajamas to watch television. Maybe watching *Minors in Malibu* reruns would make her life seem even-keeled. Hottie Gabe was in the middle of sleeping with his ex-girlfriend's mother. His life was *way* more complicated.

The phone rang at exactly noon.

"Apple!" said Brooklyn. "You're there!"

"Yes, I'm here," said Apple despondently.

"Why aren't you at school? Are you sick? You sound tired. I have these vitamin B drops that really give you energy."

"You know why I'm not at school. My life is over. I didn't even think that you were still talking to me," Apple said anxiously.

"Apple, of course I'm still talking to you. I think you just lost your way for a bit. And your life is so *not* over. Don't be dramatic. My guru says that you should never be judgmental about anyone, including yourself. It's just wasted energy," Brooklyn whispered into her cell phone. Apparently, the Helicopter had given it back.

"Yeah, well, I'm sure you've heard what happened. How can my life not be over? You know that Happy is going on my mother's show today, right?"

"Yeah, she told me," said Brooklyn. "She didn't really get into much detail. But at least her dream is finally coming true. You know she's always wanted to be a guest on *The Queen of Hearts*! We should all be happy for her."

"Brooklyn!" Apple cried. "What about *me*? What am I going to do? Do you think *I* should be happy about it?"

"Listen," Brooklyn said seriously. "I really think you should try talking to Happy again."

"I don't think she'll talk to me," Apple whimpered.

"Go to her. Go talk to her in person. Don't be a coward and call her on the phone. Come on, Apple," Brooklyn prodded. "I know you can do it. You just have to think positively. If you put out positive vibes, then only positive things will come your way. You should really talk to her in person."

"I'll think about it," Apple promised.

"And remember, Apple, just breathe. If you concentrate on your breathing, you'll stop obsessing about everything else in your life. Be zen about it all. Oops! Sorry, I didn't mean to use that word. You know what I meant when I said be zen about it, right?"

"Yes, Brooklyn. Don't worry," Apple laughed lightly. "I haven't completely lost my mind. My best friend, maybe."

"Listen, Apple, I should go. I have to eat now and maybe get a few minutes of stretching in before classes start after lunch. I'll call you later, okay?"

"Thanks, Brooklyn."

"Remember, think positively! Peace and love," Brooklyn said, hanging up.

Maybe Brooklyn was right. Even though Apple had done a shitty thing, Brooklyn was still speaking to her. She still cared enough to check in on her.

Maybe Apple *should* at least attempt to be zen. Her life could be worse, after all. She watched a couple more hours of *Minors in Malibu*, thinking about her conversation with Brooklyn.

Brooklyn was probably right. She had to speak to Happy in person. But first there was one other person she knew she would eventually need to talk to. And what better time than the present? She picked up the phone and dialed the number.

"Zen?" Apple wasn't expecting Zen to answer. She had been expecting voice mail.

"Yes, who's this?" he asked.

"It's me. Apple."

"Oh, Apple, hi," he said, sounding surprised but not unfriendly.

"Am I catching you at a bad time?"

"No, actually, I was just leaving Happy's house. We skipped classes this afternoon."

"Oh. Well, I'm calling because I guess I just want to apologize from the bottom of my heart to you for what I did. I never meant to hurt anyone, especially not you or Happy. Things just got totally out of hand," Apple said quickly. The words gushed out.

"Why did you do it, Apple?" Zen asked. "I mean, if you want to tell me."

Was it better to tell Zen how she had felt? Was there any point? But she figured she had nothing to lose now.

"I just liked you, you know," Apple said.

Zen didn't respond. Apple wasn't sure if he understood what she was getting at. Or maybe he hadn't heard her.

"I *liked* you liked you," she said, trying again. "Are you still there?"

"Yes, I'm still here," he said. "I really had no idea."

"I guess I tried to show you in my own way, but I didn't do a very good job."

"I guess not," Zen said, giving a chuckle. Even Apple smiled.

"For the longest time I've had a crush on you," she confessed. "But every time I tried to talk to you about anything, it seemed to backfire. Remember when I tried to talk to you about basketball? Remember how awkward that was? And I could never be with someone who wasn't addicted to television. And I hate all sports. And I hate cars."

204

"God, Apple, I really had no idea how you felt," Zen said again, sounding confused. "So . . . you don't feel that way about me anymore?"

"No," Apple said. She was surprised. But she knew it was mostly true. "I realize we don't have anything in common. I even volunteered for the clothing drive only to spend more time with you, not out of the goodness of my heart, like you did. But that failed too," Apple said. "I'm sorry, Zen. I am. It's like my mother always says, 'Never underestimate what heartbreak can do to a girl.'"

"Does your mother really say that, or are you making that one up too?" Zen asked, but Apple could hear the smile in his voice. She started to relax.

"No, she really does say that," she answered, laughing.

"Well, thanks for calling, Apple. I just got home and I have to be somewhere pretty soon. So, I guess I'll speak to you later?" he said.

"Wait. So will you forgive me?" Apple pressed.

"Sure, I'll forgive you. Just don't ever let it happen again."

"Do you think Happy will forgive me?" Apple asked, more self-consciously.

"I'm not sure, Apple. The only one who knows that is Happy."

"Right."

"I'll see you around, Apple," he said, and hung up.

She got off the phone, slightly wounded but relieved. It hadn't been so bad. Then she saw that there was a voice-mail message. It was her mother again, telling her she was back in town, heading directly from the airport to the studio.

Apple knew she had to speak to Happy in person before the show. And she knew the one place she would definitely find her. She had to rush and get ready if she was going to make it on time to face Happy once and for all.

nineteen

"How quickly can you get a car here?" Apple asked the lady on the phone.

"How quickly do you need one?" the lady said sleepily.

"Like, in thirty minutes or less?" Apple said impatiently.

"That's cutting it a little short."

"Well, it's for Dr. Bee Bee Berg," Apple said. "And we have an account with you. She uses you guys all the time to take her to the airport and pick her up."

"The Queen of Hearts?" the lady said, suddenly perking up.

"Yes, well, I'm her daughter, and she just called and told me she forgot some very important files and she needs me to bring them to her to the studio. The show starts very soon."

"Give me a second," said the woman, and clicked at her computer keyboard. "Okay, I can do it."

"Oh, thank you, thank you, thank you!" squealed Apple. "My mother will be thrilled." She gave the woman her address, and told her to put it on her mother's account. Then she slammed down the phone, ran upstairs, ripped off her pajamas, and jumped in the shower. Her body wasn't even fully dry as she threw on some clothes.

The driver picked her up exactly thirty minutes after the call. The drive to the studio took twenty-five minutes, most of which Apple spent biting her nails. Maybe she should get her license as soon as she could after all.

When the driver dropped her off, Apple ran to the front doors.

"Do you have a pass?" asked a security guard.

"I'm Dr. Berg's daughter," she said confidently, as if he should already know this.

"Well, then, go ahead," he said, and waved her in.

She walked down the hallways and tried to remember where her mother's dressing room was. It was kind of like riding a bike—she did remember. As a child, she used to come to the studio regularly and get her makeup put on by the professionals for fun. She popped her head through a door marked "The Queen."

"Apple! Oh my goodness. What are you doing here?" her mother asked excitedly, turning around in her swivel chair. She had been getting her makeup done and was reading her notes for the show. "Hey, everyone. Have you all met my daughter, Apple?" her mother asked proudly, looking to the makeup person, the hair person, and the wardrobe lady.

Her mother's smiled suddenly disappeared. "Apple, is everything okay? How did you get here? Are you all right? Did something happen?"

"Mom! Calm down. I'll explain later how I got here."

"It's just that you *never* come here anymore. So something must be wrong. What's wrong?" her mother asked, clearly alarmed.

"Can we get a minute alone, Mom?" Apple whispered, leaning close to her mother's ear.

"Sure. Everyone, I need a minute alone with my daughter," Dr. Berg said loudly yet calmly.

The room cleared out in seconds, and Apple suddenly found that her mother intimidated her. For a moment she saw her as the rest of the world did—as an important, powerful woman and role model. And she suddenly felt like one of the thousands of viewers who wrote desperately to the Queen of Hearts. Actually, now she *was* one of them.

"What is it, Apple?" Dr. Berg asked.

Breathe, Apple, breathe.

"I just . . . I just want to say how sorry I am for how I spoke to you and how I've been treating you. I'm sorry I didn't talk to you about my problems. I'm sorry I snuck into your computer and pretended to be you. I'm sorry I thought you were the one who broke into my computer. And I'm sorry, most of all, that I didn't ask for your advice. I'm sorry, Mom. I'm sorry about *everything.*"

Apple was shocked to see her mother's eyes tear up. She sat down on her mother's chair, almost on her lap, resting her head on her mother's shoulder. It was the closest she'd been to her mother in God knew how long.

"Oh, Apple," her mother started to say. "You're going to make me cry, and Deirdre just finished my eyes."

Apple gave a soft laugh. "I am truly sorry, Mom," she said.

"Apple, it's okay. I forgive you. I was fifteen once too, you know. I know it's hard to believe, but I was," her mother said. "So you know what the show is about today, I'm assuming. And you know who's going to be on?"

"I know, Mom. I know," Apple said gloomily.

"Well, I can put a stop to this right now, Apple. I can do that."

"Forget it. I deserve it," Apple said.

"I'm not sure you deserve *this*," Dr. Berg said giving her daughter a pointed look.

"Well, Happy has wanted to be a guest on your show forever. This is her dream come true," Apple said. "I really can't take that away from her. *Especially* after everything I did to her."

Just then, there was a sharp knock at the door and Guy walked in.

"Apple! What are you doing here? Are you here to give your friend support? That's sweet. And Guy sees that your very presence here has shocked your mother into tears! That's not good, Apple. She's got to look television perfect. So, are we ready to go on air, Mrs. Queen of Hearts?" Guy asked. "Guy's going to get Deirdre back in here to fix that mascara mess of yours. You don't want to look like a raccoon!"

"No, no. I'm fine. I'm more than fine," Dr. Berg said. "And, Guy, it's waterproof mascara! I could go swimming and it wouldn't run." She turned to face her daughter. "Are you okay, Apple?"

"I'm feeling a bit better," Apple said.

"All right then, showtime!" Guy said, clapping his hands like a boot camp instructor. "Apple, why don't you wait in the green room? Have some of those chocolate chip cookies. They are to die for."

Dr. Berg hugged her daughter and let Guy lead her out to the stage. In a few minutes, Apple thought, my life will be officially over. She felt strangely calm. What Happy would say was out of her hands, but at least her mother knew that she hadn't meant to be rotten. All I can do now is watch, she thought. She walked back to the green room and sat down on a couch facing the television.

Dr. Berg introduced the show topic—"Why Teenagers' Love Lives Are Just as Complicated as Ours"—and then invited her first guest out onstage. Apple watched Happy, her ex-best friend, walk out onstage. Apple had always known that Happy was beautiful, but she'd had no idea how super-photogenic she was until she saw her on screen.

"So, Happy, you are in tenth grade. Do you have a boyfriend?" asked Dr. Berg.

"Yes, I do. He's great," Happy said.

Apple leaned closer to the television. Had Happy just said Zen was her boyfriend? She'd had no idea their relationship had progressed so quickly.

"And how long have you two been dating?" Apple's mother asked Happy.

"Well, not very long. But we had some complications," Happy said.

"And what do you mean by that?" Dr. Bee Bee Berg asked.

"Well, another girl at my school tried to sabotage

my relationship," Happy answered, looking straight into the camera. Happy was born to be on television.

Apple felt her heart sink as the studio audience booed. Everything Apple had feared would happen was happening. It was like watching a car accident in progress. She blinked back tears. It was all going down. Right now.

"And it was my so-called best friend who tried to sabotage my relationship," Happy added. Again the audience booed. Clearly, Happy, who had watched *Queen of Hearts with Dr. Bee Bee Berg* a thousand times, knew what to say to push the audience's buttons. Even Apple couldn't help but be impressed through her own mortification. Happy was really good at this TV thing.

"What exactly do you mean by 'sabotage?'" Dr. Berg asked.

"Well, I told my friend that I liked this guy and I asked her to ask him some things to find out if he liked me too," Happy began. "And instead of doing that, she led him to believe that I wasn't a serious relationship person. Then she gave him bad advice about how to impress me. And other things like that."

"What else, dear?" Dr. Berg asked. Even though her mother knew it was Apple that Happy was talking about, she was still a professional.

"Well, she told him to not ask me to the school dance," Happy explained.

Again the audience oohed, which just egged Happy on. She was on fire.

"She told him that he should wait and that he would

seem over-eager if he asked me. Meanwhile, she knew that I wanted him to ask me. Then another guy asked me, and I so did not want to go with him, but my friend—sorry, my *ex*-friend—told me I should accept *his* invitation."

"Nooo!" the audience yelled out.

"Yes!" Happy said, looking directly into the studio. "And then she went and asked the guy *I* liked to the dance *herself*."

"Nooo!" the audience screamed.

"And how did you find all this out, dear?" Dr. Berg asked Happy.

"By accidental e-mail," Happy said simply. "My friend—my *ex*-friend—had actually written *you*, Dr. Berg, an e-mail asking you for your advice after all she did, and she accidentally sent it to *me* instead."

"Nooo!" the audience screamed again.

"Yes!" Happy said. "Sometimes the truth is stranger than fiction. But it all happened."

"And do you still talk to this friend of yours?" Dr. Berg asked.

"No. After I found out what she did, I just cut off all contact. I'm not sure I can ever trust her again," Happy said.

"Well, viewers," said Dr. Berg, turning to the camera, "as you can see, relationship problems start early. When we come back, we'll hear from Happy if she plans to ever forgive her friend."

The television in the green room went black. The commercials were not aired in the green room like they were at home. Apple thought she was for sure in shock because her hands felt frozen. In fact, her whole body felt frozen.

Her cell phone started to ring. Apple picked it up.

"You are so screwed," the voice said teasingly. It was Aunt Hazel.

"I know! I'm never going to be able to show my face again," muttered Apple.

"Come on! I was joking. It wasn't that bad," Aunt Hazel said.

"Are you serious?" Apple asked. "Was it really not that bad?" Maybe it just seemed so bad to Apple because she knew Happy was talking about her. Maybe it didn't seem so bad to all the other viewers. Maybe the rest of the world was mainly concentrating on how beautiful Happy looked.

"No, it *was* sort of bad," said Aunt Hazel, sympathetically. "I'm just being honest."

"What am I going to do?" Apple moaned.

"Where are you?" Aunt Hazel asked. "I'm at your place and you're not here. Aren't you grounded?"

"I'm at the studio," Apple told her.

"You are not!"

"I am!"

"What are you doing there?" her aunt asked.

"I thought I'd try to get some face time with Happy before it all went down."

"I guess that didn't exactly work out," Aunt Hazel said.

"No, I didn't get a chance to see her. But I did make up with my mother, at least. Oh, God, I'll never be able to show my face anywhere ever again," she moaned.

"You'd better get out of there, Apple. I mean, if that

studio audience finds out that you are the one to have caused all that trouble, you'll be lynched to pieces."

"I know! I never thought I'd ever be saying this, Aunt Hazel," Apple began, "but I really, really need your advice. What can I do?"

"Well, I guess there is *one* thing you can do. But it is a pretty *brave* thing."

"Just tell me. I'll do anything," cried Apple.

"It's something that not even in my craziest moments would I ever do myself," Aunt Hazel warned. "And you know how crazy I can be."

"I don't have time for this! Just tell me already," Apple demanded.

Crazy Aunt Hazel told Apple her plan. It *was* crazy. It was the craziest plan Apple had ever heard. But what other choice did she have now?

twenty

$a$pple took a deep breath and walked out onstage, blinking in the glare of the studio lights. She was daunted by the cameras, by the audience, by seeing Happy. She knew she was paying for her sins. She was sacrificing all her much-loved privacy at this moment, and she was shaking like a leaf. Her mother was in the middle of asking Happy another question when she noticed Apple walking toward them. Apple concentrated on her mother and Happy and tried to ignore the hundreds of pairs of eyes staring at her from the studio audience.

"Apple!" her mother said, standing up. Even her mother's unfailing professionalism was shaken. She looked shocked. But she quickly composed herself, plastered a smile on her face, and turned to the studio audience. "Everyone, I'd like to introduce you to Apple. My daughter."

The audience clapped and hooted, which made

Apple feel even more nervous. She didn't like to be the center of attention.

Apple glanced at Happy, who looked more pissed off than surprised. As the audience continued to clap, her mother leaned in and whispered in Apple's ear. "What are you doing?" she asked.

"I need to say something," she whispered back. "Here. Now."

"You do understand that we're live here!" her mother said a little more loudly.

"Yes, Mom! I know how the show works. I need to say what I have to say *on air.*"

"Okay," her mother said, throwing her arms up and stepping back.

As the audience calmed down, Dr. Berg called out to them. "Well, this is quite the surprise. I didn't expect this. Can we get my daughter a microphone please?"

A soundman ran up and hooked a microphone onto Apple's collar. Usually the wire would go under the shirt to hide it, but there was no time now for presentation. Her mother directed her to sit on the couch next to Happy. Happy sat up taller and looked straight ahead to the audience.

"Apple," her mother said. "Tell us what you're doing out here . . . turning up in the middle of the show today."

"I'd just like to say that I'm the one who tried to sabotage her relationship," Apple admitted quietly. She could hear her voice shaking. "The girl Happy was talking about is me."

The audience, as she had expected, started oohhing

and ahhing. To Apple it seemed as loud as a plane flying right through the studio. She started to feel disoriented.

Apple started to speak again while the audience was still hollering. She had the urge to yell at them, "Let me explain!" But she turned to Happy.

"I'm just here because I need you, Happy, to know how sorry I am. I never meant to hurt you. You've been my best friend forever. And you know how hard this is for me," Apple said to her.

Happy looked down at her hands, which were clasped in her lap.

"Is this true, Happy?" Dr. Bee Bee Berg asked. "Do you think this is hard for Apple?"

"Yes, I do," Happy admitted. "We call her the Sponge, because she never talks about her feelings. Not even to her friends or family."

"Apple, can you tell us why you did this? I know this is hard," her mother said, "but we all need to fully understand this."

"Yes, it is hard. But I want to. I liked Happy's now-boyfriend for years, *before* he got so cute," she said, looking again at her friend. For a brief moment, Apple forgot that they were sitting in front of a live studio audience and that millions of people were watching them in their homes.

"But you never said anything," Happy said to her.

"I know. I really don't know how to talk about my feelings. I just couldn't," Apple said, her voice continuing to waver. "But I'd like to try now."

There was a moment of silence. Happy looked like

she was deep in thought.

"And can you believe she is my daughter? My own flesh and blood?" Dr. Bee Bee Berg interrupted, looking out to the audience, who laughed obediently. "So what else exactly do you have to say to Happy?" her mother asked, turning her attention back to Apple.

"Just that I wonder if she could ever forgive me and that I love her and that I promise to try and talk more openly about my feelings," Apple said quickly, and added, "if she'd be willing to listen."

"Now, this boy, whom you, Apple, liked and who is now Happy's boyfriend," her mother said. "Do you still have feelings for him?"

The audience was stone silent. Apple felt a heaviness in her chest, like someone was pounding on her heart. It was a fair question, she guessed. Happy raised her eyebrows expectantly.

"No, I don't think so," Apple said. "No, I *know* I don't. I just want to be friends with Happy again. That's all I want. No guy is worth losing Happy over," Apple added, and she meant it.

"Do you want my advice, people?" Dr. Bee Bee Berg said to the studio audience.

The audience screamed out in unison, "Yes, we want your advice, Queen of Hearts!"

Happy still refused to look at Apple. Here I am, thought Apple, onstage, answering questions about the most personal details of my life, admitting what I did in front of millions of people, begging Happy for forgiveness, and it may all backfire. This was a crazy plan. *Happy may never forgive me*, she thought.

"I think, Apple, you'll have to earn Happy's trust back." Dr. Berg turned to Apple, saying more quietly, "I know it's harsh, and trust me, there's no one in the world I'd like to see this work out for more than you, but you have to *earn* trust," she said.

"And how do I do that?" Apple asked.

"Baby steps, as always. Baby steps. It takes time to heal all wounds, especially trust wounds. But you have a history, and a good history, with Happy. I'd start by having a heart-to-heart. Get it all out on the table. Share your feelings. Really listen to one another. Everyone makes mistakes, and sometimes trust is about faith. Apple, you may have to trust that Happy will take that leap of faith and believe in you again. Happy, does that sound about right to you?" her mother asked.

Finally, Happy looked at Apple.

"Yes. I *would* like to be friends again with Apple. I mean, she's been my best friend for years," Happy said. "It may take some time, but I'm sure we'll get there."

Happy stood up, much to Apple's surprise, and hugged her. The audience clapped wildly. It was a TV moment made in heaven. Apple looked up and saw Guy wiping a tear from his eye in the director's booth on the second floor, and mouthing the words, "Brava! Brava!"

Apple felt her mother shoving something in her hand. It was a Kleenex. Two seconds later, Apple really started to cry—but these were tears of relief, letting it all out. How was it that her mother always knew when her guests were going to break down?

twenty-one

"I can't believe you're doing this," Aunt Hazel said as she pulled up to the curb. Dr. Bee Bee Berg and her father were out on a date night. "You are so much braver than I am. I would have moved cities and gotten a whole new identity!"

"Well, after what I did yesterday, I think I can pretty much do anything, don't you?" Apple asked. "I mean, if I could get up and cry and admit to the world what I did, I can certainly walk into a school dance," Apple said. But she didn't feel as confident as her words. Maybe this *is* a bad idea, she thought. Maybe her aunt was right.

"Who would have thought you had it in you?" asked Aunt Hazel.

"Not me," Apple said. "But it was your bright idea. So thank you. Maybe I should really listen to you more often about relationships."

"Are you kidding me? He dumped me!"

"That guy you were dating? The one you had three fantastic dates with," Apple said sympathetically.

"Yup. Apparently, he's just not 'ready' for a serious relationship. God, if I hear that line one more time . . ."

Apple felt bad for her aunt, but she was too nervous about getting out to really concentrate on her words.

"Who's that cute man?" Aunt Hazel asked suddenly, oblivious to Apple's hesitation.

"Who?" Apple asked.

"That guy over there!" Crazy Aunt Hazel said, tapping on the window.

"That's Mr. Kelly," Apple said. "He must be a chaperone."

"The famous math teacher!" her aunt exclaimed.

"Well, he's not famous," said Apple. "It was a fake diary entry, remember?"

"But you're right, Apple. He is cute. Very cute," her aunt said. "You have good taste in older men."

"Hey! That was a *made up problem*! Gross! I so do not think he's cute!" Apple insisted.

"Well, I certainly do. Introduce us," Aunt Hazel demanded.

"No way! You really are crazy!"

"Oh come on, Apple. Do me this one favor? Please? I'm desperate here, and he's cute!" her aunt begged. "I helped you with your problem. You owe me."

"I can't believe I'm going to do this!" Apple said, unbuckling her seatbelt.

"Hurry up! He's going in," her aunt cried, leaning over and opening the passenger door and pushing Apple out.

"Okay, pushy much?" Apple said. Mr. Kelly was just opening the front door of the school.

"Hey, Mr. Kelly! Wait up!" Apple called, racing up to him.

"Apple! Well, I just saw you on television the other day," Mr. Kelly said when she was in front of him. "And Happy too! I can't believe that two of my students were on *The Queen of Hearts!* It was pretty fascinating, even for an old man like me. I'm so glad I'm not a fifteen-year-old girl! My goodness, what drama!"

Oh, God. Did everyone in the world watch her mother's show? If Mr. Kelly did, then the answer must be yes.

"Right. Anyway," Apple said, pretending not to hear him, "there's someone who wants to meet you."

"Your mother? Did Dr. Bee Bee Berg drop you off?" he said excitedly, looking past Apple toward the row of cars.

"Well, no. It's not exactly my mother. But it's the next best thing," Apple said, trying to sell up her aunt.

"I'm intrigued," Mr. Kelly said, tapping his fingers together. "Where is this mystery person?"

"Over there," Apple said, pointing to her aunt's car. "It's my aunt. She's single and desperate."

Mr. Kelly looked at Apple.

"I was joking," she said. "But she *is* single. She saw you and she thinks you're cute and wants to meet you."

"Interesting," Mr. Kelly said. "So what should I do?"

"Um, just go over and say 'hi.'" Apple said. It seemed like only hours ago that she was sabotaging relationships, and now people were expecting her to be a matchmaker?

Guy was right: people's memories were short. Mr. Kelly seemed to already have moved on from seeing Apple and Happy on the show. She could only hope that her fellow students would be as forgetful.

She watched as Mr. Kelly headed over to the car. She saw her aunt open the door and jump out. She watched them shake hands and start to chat.

Then Apple took a deep breath and walked into the school and into the large gymnasium, which was decorated all in red. There were red streamers and red balloons. It looked like a can of red paint had exploded. She heard the whispers as she walked by, everything from "That's her! That's the one!" to "Keep her away from my boyfriend" to "How could she show her face? I could never!"

"You know why people are interested in my show?" her mother had asked her earlier that day when Apple was debating whether to go to the dance or not. "It's because they're not happy in their own relationships. If people are that interested in yours, it means nothing good is happening in theirs. And remember, Apple—the only people who really know what's going on in a relationship are the two people who are in it. And that goes for friendships, too. People may not understand why you did what you did, or they may not understand how Happy and Zen could forgive you, but only you and Happy really know what's going on between you."

Apple walked to the back of the gymnasium, trying to hold her head high.

"Hey, Apple, how's your pie?" Hopper asked as Apple walked by him.

At least some things never changed. Hopper was still Hopper. *He* wasn't treating her any differently.

"God, Hopper. Can you grow up?" Apple asked.

"Hey, be nice to my date," Brooklyn said, popping up behind him.

"He's *your* date?" Apple asked, shocked. She looked at Hopper, then back at Brooklyn. "Let me get this straight. Hopper is your date? You like Hopper?"

"Yes! I've liked him for a while. You're not the only one with secrets, Apple," said Brooklyn. "I just know how to release stress better. It's called *yoga*."

"And I suddenly found myself dateless at the last minute," Hopper said. "I think you know why, Apple—Happy called and bailed on me."

"Okay, I deserve that," Apple said.

"Hey!" Brooklyn said, swatting him on the arm. "I thought you were thrilled to be going with me!"

"I'm just joking, my little yogi. You know that. In fact, I should really thank Apple for doing what she did. Because I now have the cutest date ever. You know that I always really wanted to go with you from the start, Brooklyn. I just didn't know how to ask a person who spends more time lying flat on her back on the floor than walking. But I'm sure I can grow to get used to your peace and love ways. Now, since you aren't on a yoga mat flat on the floor at present, come dance with me," Hopper said, pulling Brooklyn by her arm.

Hopper and Brooklyn? Well, Apple thought, stranger things have happened. And it's like her mother had said: no one knows what goes on in a relationship except the two people in it. Maybe it would work out for Hopper and Brooklyn.

She watched her fellow classmates around her laughing and dancing, and felt out of place. Would anyone want to be seen with her, let alone ask her to dance?

Happy and Zen were dancing in the middle of the room. Happy looked like an angel, in a white dress. And Zen, Apple had to admit, still looked super hot. She watched as they wrapped their arms around each other. She felt a pang, even if he wasn't her Zen Crush anymore.

As if they could feel Apple's eyes on them, they both looked in her direction. Apple looked down. She still couldn't look them in the eye. She would have to work on that.

Apple glanced up again and saw Happy and Zen coming toward her. They were holding hands. Apple felt only a small kick in the gut. They looked, she had to admit, like the perfect couple.

Apple knew that everyone had started watching them, wondering what would happen. But she didn't really care. She only wondered what Happy would say to her. They hadn't spoken since they had hugged on *Queen of Hearts*. When the show had ended, Happy had managed to sneak out while Apple was talking to her mother.

"Hey, Apple. You look gorgeous," Happy said, giving Apple another hug.

Apple was about to argue, but she stopped herself. She needed to learn to just be confident again.

"Thanks, Happy. So do you—as always" she said. "Hi, Zen."

"Hey, Apple. Great party, huh? Glad you made it," he said.

"Me too," Apple said. She meant it.

"So, Apple, I have a question for you," Happy said.

Apple felt her stomach drop. "Yes?" she asked. Were they going to get back into everything that Apple had done?

"Is that your Aunt Hazel over there dancing with Mr. Kelly?" Happy asked.

"What?" Apple shrieked. "Where?"

Apple turned her head toward the spot Happy was pointing at. Sure enough, there was her Crazy Aunt Hazel slow-dancing with Mr. Kelly. Her aunt was resting her head on Mr. Kelly's shoulder and Mr. Kelly had his hand on the small of her aunt's back.

"Oh my God," Apple said, looking back at Happy. "Oh my God!"

They burst out laughing. It had been so long since Apple had laughed like that. Brooklyn walked over with Hopper and joined them.

"What are you guys laughing about?" Brooklyn asked.

Happy and Apple looked at each other and burst out laughing again.

"What, you guys? What?" Brooklyn insisted. "You're not laughing because I'm with Hopper, are you? I know I should have told you guys sooner that I liked him. Okay, I like him. Fine, I've liked him for a long time. Now you know everything!"

Happy and Apple looked at Brooklyn and then at each other and burst out laughing yet again.

"Don't be so paranoid, Brooklyn," Happy finally said.

In a giggling fit, Apple pointed toward her aunt and Mr. Kelly.

"Look!" Happy said. "Over there! That's what we're laughing at. But," she added, "I'm glad you told us about Hopper."

"No!" said Brooklyn. "Is that who I think it is? Is that Crazy Aunt Hazel?"

"Yup!" laughed Apple.

"How did that happen?" Brooklyn asked.

"All I know is when we got here, Crazy Aunt Hazel thought he was cute and asked me to introduce them. I have no idea how they wound up like *that*!" Apple said, wiping her eyes. "But my aunt does move quickly."

"I'll say she does. Well, maybe you are a better matchmaker than you seemed," Happy said. "Maybe it's not always so bad when you meddle."

Apple and Happy exchanged looks, but it was okay. Or at least Apple knew it *would* be okay, one day soon enough.

Apple felt other eyes on her. Sure enough there was a guy hovering around them.

"Oh, right. Apple, speaking of introductions, have you met Lyon? He's a friend of Sailor's. He wanted to meet you," Happy said, waving Lyon over.

"Me? Why me?" Apple asked.

"Oh, he'll tell you," she said.

Happy made the quick introduction. "Apple, this is Lyon. Lyon, this is Apple."

They shook hands.

"Hey," Apple said.

"Hey," Lyon said.

"Well, I'm going to go dance," said Happy. "Let's go, Zen. Catch you later, Apple?"

"Absolutely," Apple said.

"We're going out there too," said Brooklyn, holding onto Hopper. "Have fun, Apple!"

Suddenly Apple was alone with Lyon. She had seen him around, but they had never spoken, in large part because he was older.

"So," said Lyon. "Having fun?"

"I guess so," Apple said. She suddenly felt very thirsty. Her mouth was dry.

"Well, I've seen you around," said Lyon.

"I've seen you around too," Apple answered.

"But then I just happened to be at home the other day and my sister had on *Queen of Hearts*, and I *really* saw you," Lyon said.

"Oh, God, that. I guess everyone saw it," Apple moaned.

"Hey! I didn't mean to upset you. I thought you were very brave," he said. "I thought what you did was awesome."

Apple looked at him. He seemed to be sincere. He didn't seem to be making fun of her.

"Really?" she said. "Because most people would have thought what I had done was really crappy. It *was* really crappy."

"No, not what you did, but what you did *about* it. Most people would never have admitted it if they had done something like that, and so publicly. I think it's very admirable," Lyon said. "I think *you* think you came off way worse than you actually did."

"Thanks, I think," said Apple.

"Take it as a compliment," he said. "I was very impressed. And you looked really pretty too," he added. "And that's important in television-land."

Apple felt her lips turning up in a smile. Who was this guy who was making her smile and even feel at ease?

"So, do you want to dance?" Lyon asked.

"Yes, I very much would like to dance," Apple answered.

"Great," he said, holding out his hand to take hers. "Let's go."

"Oh, but there's just one thing," Apple said, pausing.

"What?" he asked, looking a little worried.

"Just let's stay away from that area over there, where Mr. Kelly is dancing," Apple said.

"Mr. Kelly? Why?" Lyon asked.

"Because he's dancing with my Crazy Aunt Hazel," she explained.

"With whom?" Lyon asked.

"It's a long story," Apple said, gazing up at Lyon. He was quite handsome. She could start fresh with Lyon, she thought.

"Well, the night is young," he said. "I hope there will be plenty of time for you to tell me everything about this woman you call Crazy Aunt Hazel. And maybe a bit about you."

"Yes," Apple agreed, smiling up at him. "The night is young."

♡   •

Dear ED,

I'm so glad to be writing to you again. I've missed you! I've decided to trust people a little more and go back to writing to you, ED, my dear electronic diary. So, Aunt Hazel, if you are reading this, just stop it right now. You know how wrong it is. And be forewarned. I will be writing about you! So if you don't want to know my honest thoughts, don't read any further. Well, ED, I just got back from the Valentine Ball. And it wasn't awful. In fact, it was almost awesome. Happy and I are going to be okay. We made plans to go to Gossip together next week. I'm not saying we're back to where we were just yet, but I'm hopeful. I wonder if I can ever get over what I did? I just do not ever want to end up in that place again. Also, Brooklyn admitted she likes Hopper. Hopper! Who knows why we like the people we do? Speaking of which, Crazy Aunt Hazel was seen leaving the school dance, looking very cozy with Mr. Kelly. Forget about him being a chaperone tonight. He sucked at being a chaperone. He was too busy sucking my aunt's face. I saw them, along with many others, when I was leaving in the parking lot. Remind me to thank Crazy Aunt Hazel for that—all my classmates started talking about Mr. Kelly kissing some lady, and stopped staring at and whispering about me. The spare bedroom, too, I noticed, was empty again tonight, which means my parents are sleeping together again. That's something else I don't really want to think about. But it means they are getting along, at least. And my mother was so proud of me after I went on her show! I'm not sure if it's because I finally opened up, and in such a dramatic way, or because Guy told her afterward that it was one of the highest-rated shows they've had in months. I don't really want to think about how many people saw me cry on television. What I do want to think about is Lyon. Happy introduced us tonight, and we spent the next couple of hours together basically just talking and laughing. And he asked me out! My first real date! I'm so nervous. But I'm going to be ME. For better or worse, I'm going to be myself and follow my mother's advice about not playing games. I also received an interesting e-mail from an editor at *B-Grrl Magazine*— only the best magazine out there!—who says she might want to use me as a professional advice columnist for the magazine. I'd get paid and everything! She, of course, watched me on *The Queen of Hearts*. So more than one good thing came out of that whole crazy plan. In her e-mail, it says she believes I'd be the perfect person to dole out advice, since I've probably learned from my mistakes and also since I'm the daughter of the Queen of Hearts. Me? Giving professional advice and getting paid for it? Can you imagine, ED? Maybe I AM my mother's daughter after all!